REALITY, REALITY

ALSO BY JACKIE KAY

Red Dust Road
Wish I Was Here
Why Don't You Stop Talking
Trumpet

Poetry
Fiere
The Lamplighter
Darling
Life Mask
Off Colour
Other Lovers
The Adoption Papers

JACKIE KAY

REALITY, REALITY

PICADOR

First published 2012 by Picador
an imprint of Pan Macmillan, a division of Macmillan Publishers Limited
Pan Macmillan, 20 New Wharf Road, London N1 9RR
Basingstoke and Oxford
Associated companies throughout the world
www.panmacmillan.com

ISBN 978-1-4472-1756-5

A CIP catalogue record for this book is available from
the British Library.

Typeset by SetSystems Ltd, Saffron Walden, Essex
Printed and bound by CPI Group (UK) Ltd, Croydon, CR0 4YY

For Denise Else

We writers may think we invent too much –
but reality is worse
every time.

FLAUBERT

It really happened in really real life.

ALI SMITH

Contents

Reality, Reality

Now that – that is bursting with flavour. I'm getting ginger, and then I'm getting lime coming in at the end there. That is a sensation. That is delicious. I could eat up the whole plate. Today, I told myself I was going to have a positive day. Today was day one of My Big Week. I got up early and scrubbed the face with cold water. I was shallow of breath due to the excitement. I couldn't stop talking to myself. I couldn't quieten down. Here's the voice, going duh duh duh duh duhhh non-stop. *Can you win? Have you got what it takes? Are you going to shoot yourself in the foot? Get egg on your face? Hmmmmmn? Only the extremely talented survive. It's all about separating the wheat from the chaff. Only the ones with that special extra ingredient, sorrowful as sorrel, mysterious as saffron, wise as sage, magic as a glittering sheet of gelatine, only the crème de la crème rises to the surface! COOKING doesn't GET tougher THAN this!* I was shouting now into the mirror. Big voice! Big flavours! I rinsed the face, enthusiastically again and again and again. I dabbed the face dry and confessed soberly to my dark-eyed reflection: *We're looking for elegance.*

But truth be told, I was feeling a bit ropy on

account of drinking too much whisky the night before. I've been drinking whisky because it's good exercise for my palate. Me drinking a different whisky is like an artist trying a new colour. It's part of my culinary training, sniffing and detecting. This one was a top dram – 73.32 – and, just to perfect my expertise, I sniffed several times and swirled before saying to myself, 'Stef, what can you smell?' I was watching my *24* box set and I turned it down because Jack Bauer was putting me off my stride. I can smell polished wood, polished wood and maybe pear drops. Suddenly, there was Ali and me sharing sweets in the park with the burn near the house I grew up in. I had pear drops and she had Italian creams, which only our Italian cafe seemed to do, exquisite sweets – a kind of fudge with a thick, dark chocolate bottom – and we both had shining eyes, girls' eyes, excited to be in each other's company. Maybe that's it; it's downhill all the way from then. There's nothing like the old excitement of girls. Where did they go, the old pals of the babbling brook, and I was swirling the whisky and getting a kind of crème brûlée flavour sneaked in at the end, or maybe vanilla custard. I had three doubles to be sure. Yep. Orange peels and vanilla custard. Then I staggered up the steep stairs to bed, and the whisky roared me to sleep. It wasn't a lullaby. It was loud, a sailor singing *speed bonny boat* at the top of his voice. Finally, I think I landed up on Skye and fell asleep remembering the time when I went to the south of Skye on holiday, a cottage near the

Aird of Sleat, and I met a man who said, 'Have you been to the north of the island?' I said, 'Yes,' and he said, 'I dinna like it up there, it's much too commercialized.' And he was talking about three shops! Or the time when I was in a pub in Orkney and England was playing Germany and England was winning four to one, would you believe, and a wee man's voice shouted out, 'C'mon, Germany!' and everyone laughed. I went to sleep thinking about that, and my big day, which is now today. I said, 'C'mon, Stef! You've some day ahead. Get yourself some shut-eye, do yourself a favour.'

Well, so here we are on the first day of My Big Week, and I'm absolutely determined to excel. But first things first! Feed the dog breakfast! I haven't yet stretched to gourmet meals for my mutt, so I get out a tin and open it, absolutely no point sniffing the tin for notes of offal. It's an awful smell, pet food. I take the dog round the block. Can't wait to get back to my kitchen! I've got a stopwatch, a set of kitchen scales, a new KitchenAid, a heavy-bottomed pot, a sharp knife, a good chopping board. Cost me a wee fortune, but money well spent. It cost much less than the five-day trip to Florence I'd been thinking about, or the seven days to Lake Garda. I reckon I'm bang on the money: holiday at home is the new going away. Going anywhere nice? somebody at work asked me. I'm having a staycation, I said. I've taken a week off work. Well, I'm sick of paying a single supplement to go on holiday on my own. I mean what nonsense! Hello? Pay extra for a single bed? Huh? What kind of person thought that up? Did they sit down one afternoon with a cup of tea, and think to themselves, Aha! Let the recently bereaved, the dumped, the chucked and the lonely pay more, they're a waste of space? Don't get me started! One of the reasons I'm putting myself through the HEATS is to see if the HEATS might control my RANTS and stop me veering off the subject. Focus, Chef Stef, this is what is asked of you today. Extreme focus; absolute commitment. You've got twenty minutes. There is absolutely no room for error. *Let's Cook!* – the voice of the greasy-haired one. I am good at doing his voice. I frighten myself with my own brilliant mimicry! Talk about intimidating. *Let's Cook!*

Timer set for twenty minutes, no cheating. Twenty minutes exactly. Was tempted to give myself twenty-three, but what's the point in cheating on myself? It's like pretending to the weighing scales you've lost more than you've lost. The scales know and so do you. I crack three eggs on the dot of twenty and swiftly whisk them. (I might develop upper-arm muscles as a side benefit.) I chop mushrooms, parsley, and red onion. I roast a red pepper. *Ten minutes!* I grate some Gruyère cheese, and slice some soda bread. I sauté the mushrooms and the parsley and the red onion together. *Five minutes!* I grill the tomatoes. I skin and then slice the red pepper. They are all ready! I slip the eggs into the pan and cook on a medium to hot heat, then I add the separate ingredients and fold over. *Thirty seconds! Plate up!* I stand back from my plate, quickly, sneakily, sprinkling parsley over the omelette as my timer rings. *Stand back from your bench! Time's up!* I was out of breath. OMG, it all mattered so much!

I sit down at my table, ten thirty a.m., a little later than planned, to eat the first HEAT meal of the day. I've made a fresh pot of Earl Grey tea, fresh leaves, note, not tea bags, sniff, and some soda-bread toast. I don't have time to look at the morning newspaper and see what's going on in the world. I'm sweating, anxious, about what is going to be said. *You've played it safe with an omelette*, the fat-faced friendly one says. *To be honest, I'm a little disappointed. And what a lot of work you gave yourself. Nice, but not very inspiring. Where's the flamboyancy in an omelette?* Ah but what an omelette, the greasy-haired one says. *This must be the best omelette I have ever eaten in my entire life!* As he enthuses, I realize it's his approval I want most of all. *I'm getting the Gruyère flavour, that lovely warm roast red pepper.* I suddenly sink and flag, the air going out of me like an imperfect soufflé. I'm depressed with my lack of ambition. An omelette! Call yourself a chef, Stef, and that's what you produce for the semi-finals? You better smarten up, girl, or you're going home. *The Girl needs to push herself. The Girl needs to raise her game.* I need to get to the shops, pronto, for lunch and dinner's ingredients. Some holiday this is turning out to be! Walkies, I say to my dog, who is the only one who seems to listen to me these days. She wags her tail and sits by the front door whilst I double-check things. Now, now, Stef, think positive, you can still turn yourself around. There's still time for self-improvement. I try to walk fast, but I can't walk fast because I'm carrying fifteen stone, which since I tried my new 'Whisky Diet' is a lot less than I was a few weeks ago, when I was sixteen and a half stone, before I was promoted to the semi-finals. Low carbs – that's the secret. That's why the whisky is a necessity. No carbohydrates in whisky. Little-known fact, that. People out there don't know the difference between carbs and calories, but don't get me started.

I walk into my local fish shop, Out of the Blue. I know they know I live alone. If you buy one tuna steak on a Wednesday and one red mullet on a Thursday and splash out and buy one sushi and one piece of halibut on a Saturday, there's no hiding the absolute extent of your aloneness. Sometimes the man throws in tails of organically smoked haddock out of sympathy. Once he gave me a free free-range chicken which had lost both its legs, but other than that was in pretty good nick. Didn't chickens used to fly? I couldn't tell if it lost its legs whilst still alive or not. Don't let's go there. I buy a piece of halibut and a hake steak in Out of the Blue; some fresh spinach, rocket, pear and hazelnuts in the Unicorn, a small piece of Gorgonzola in the Barbican. It seems silly facing the long queue and taking my number, number thirty-four, for four ounces of Gorgonzola but I am emphatic about sticking to my chosen ingredients. A lot of people veer dramatically away from the shopping list; not me.

I take my dog through the Beech Road park and on the way back I bump into another dog owner who is in quite a state. I don't know her name but I know her dog's. She says, 'I can't remember when I last got Gatsby wormed. I'm not sure if it's April she's due or now. If it's April I'd rather wait, last year I kept a diary. A dog diary!' She laughs at herself like she is some kind of genius – 'But I forgot, and chucked it out, not thinking I'd need to check the dates for this year.' She throws her eyes up in the air like she is tossing a ball for her dog to fetch, and then she walks off. I am getting used to my only real intimacy coming from the confessions of dog-walkers. It's amazing the things people tell me. A man stopped to chat the other day, a complete stranger with a Great Dane. He pointed to the slobbering big-eyed dog and said, 'She gets jealous if I get a new woman. She's driven all the girls out, even the missus. She's the missus now, eh, eh?' I couldn't tell if he was proud or defeated. He shrugged his shoulders then he hurried off through the woods that lead you to the river Mersey, which stretches all the way from here to Liverpool.

Today, I've really not got time to stand about chatting to dog-owners. 'I'm up against the clock,' I say and hurry past the woman who usually stops whilst out walking her Scottish terrier and her Zimmer. 'Okay,' she says, her hands resting on the Zimmer. 'Nice day today!' 'Lovely, yes,' I say. 'Doing anything nice?' she says. 'I'm cooking cordon bleu! I'm in the semi-finals!' I tell her. She's the first person I've told. 'It's costing me more than the vet, all the expensive ingredients, but worth it!' 'Mmmm,' she says and looks a bit envious, or is it dubious, I'm not sure. I bid her farewell. For all I know the heights of her culinary expectations are a tin of Heinz Tomato Soup, followed by a tin of Ambrosia Creamed Rice.

Stop it, Chef Stef! You've turned into a well big snob since you were picked for the semi-finals! I hope you're not going to leave your old friends behind? Of course not! I hurry through the small park with my Tibetan terrier following behind me. The tender yellow and purple crocuses are out and the modest white snowdrops. My dog stops to sniff the crocuses, pisses, then sniffs again (her equivalent to Chanel No. 5). The shy spring is here. What a relief! The trees are still bare but the leaves will be coming. I hope the schnauzer we often bump into is not coming out today. Damn. My dog has stopped for a poo and I get out my plastic bag. I wait for a second while it cools; it's the warmth that bothers me most. When I pick it up, I try and think of what the consistency is most like, bread dough maybe, anyone? Clootie dumpling in the pillow? – and in this way, I'm always thinking culinary thoughts even when performing a most unpleasant task. This, as it were, allows me to work on the job! I dispose of the plastic bag in the red dog bin. But the smell, I can't really stretch to comparing the smell to anything. Put it this way, it's not exactly fragrant. That's enough, Stef; let your dog have her modesty. My dog is a bit embarrassed that I have to pick up her doo-doo, because she's a pernickety wee thing. If she were to hear my inside thoughts, she'd be mortified.

I arrive back home. Nearly time to start the timer and the lunch. It is one o'clock. No time for the lunchtime news. I am the news. I am the rolling news. I have lost a stone and a half and have started my own HEATS. I could perfect my style and earn a fortune. What would I call it? *The Whisky Diet?* (That would attract fat alkies!) *You Diet and Dog Diets Too?* (That would lure obese people who uncannily resemble their obese canines.) For lunch, I'm serving a watercress soup to start followed by a lovely piece of halibut with a Welsh rarebit topping and a spinach, pine nut and raisin salad. I'm using up the Gruyère from the morning omelette. I ask myself: What are we looking for today from you, Stef, do you think? A beautiful plate of food, I answer myself. I need to cook my heart out today. Need to take risks! It is do or die today. *Let's Cook!* I'm not hungry actually, but I must stick to the gruelling schedule, or I can't call myself anything.

I mix a tablespoon of Dijon mustard, two table-spoons of double cream, a cup of grated Gruyère into a paste, spread it on my halibut and put the halibut in the oven at 200 degrees. I set my timer for twenty minutes. DO NOT OVERCOOK FISH! Then I toast the pine nuts, but burn them a little. HELP! Then I soak the raisins but for too long – they look like the wrinkled eyes of very small, very old animals, beavers maybe, or badgers. I taste my watercress soup having whizzed it through the new KitchenAid that I bought specially for this special week, and cheap at the price too in a way, less than a week on the Costa Brava, or nine nights in Morocco, which would have been nice since I love Moroccan food. No, here's me, bravely à la Costa o Solo Mio, and soon when I am truly brilliant I will be certainly inviting people CHEZ moi and certainly will stun them with my big bold flavours and elegant presentation. *Stand back from your bench! That watercress soup is so green*, the greasy-haired one says. *That is delicious*, the fat-faced friendly one says. *That green reminds you of allotments, childhood, it's as fresh as spring. I'm getting that good iron. I mean, phwoar! Phwoar!* I nod and look sage and try to hide my superior smile. I imagine the faces of the other contestants turning an envious green. *Now for the main. Presentation could be better. That spinach is looking a bit sloppy and has left a trail of water on the plate. You've let yourself down! Flavour good. Could do with more seasoning. I'm getting the sweetness of the raisins, but "those pine nuts . . ."* This fish, nice idea with the Welsh rarebit topping, but a bit of a waste of a lovely fish, halibut.

I don't agree with you, I say quietly. *At this level, you need to be better. You are going home, Stef. Sorry. You're going home.* You don't know what you're talking about, I say again. You're just a jumped-up pair of idiots. You wouldn't know a good meal if it slapped you in the face. You don't even like good food! Is it because I didn't do snail porridge? Too right, I'm a bad loser! I feel myself being frogmarched round the kitchen. Some-one shouts, *Cut! Take her off set!* I can hardly breathe. Some holiday this is for me. The stress! The tension! I've failed. I haven't made the final. I haven't realized my dream. I'm devastated. Gutted like a school of snapper. The once-in-a-lifetime opportunity has slipped through my fishing net. I see myself in the sad green room, not the dream room. I'm frank with the camera. There's no way I'm stopping cooking, I say to the little light in my kitchen that is really the eye of the burglar alarm but could just as easily be the eye of the watching world. No way. I've got my dreams. I could still turn up trumps and deliver the goods. Then they'd be the ones with egg on their face, ketchup on their pants – tossers. Complete tossers. It's always the men they pick. How come the men get to be chefs and the women get to be cooks? It's a disgrace.

I take out my fine bottle of whisky. Make that a double. I've just narrowly missed the finals, whatdya expect? I was *that* close. Give me a break. Is this you drowning your sorrows, Chef Stef? Too right it is. Get it down! Pear drops? Teardrops, more like. Crème brûlée? Cry baby. I look at myself in the bathroom mirror. My face looks like a summer pudding. I've got myself all upset. A voice whispers, *You've one more chance. It doesn't involve anyone but you. Let's Cook. Come on, now, love.* It's a gentle voice, lovely, not my own. I think it sounds like the voice of my dead mother, but I can't be sure because I've forgotten her voice. I wish I could remember her voice exactly. What was it like? Like fresh spring water babbling down the Fintry hills.

It is four hours and three minutes since I last cooked, and five hours and ten minutes since I last walked the dog, and one hour and six minutes since I last had a snooze and now it is time to prove myself. My eyelids are swollen from crying, like little slugs. My face is all blotchy. But it's not about looks, being a chef, only your food needs to look beautiful really. I get out my blue and white striped apron that I bought specially, but had forgotten buying. Silly me! I tie a knot, confidently. Lucky apron. For starters, pear fried in ground coriander with hazelnuts, rocket and Gorgonzola salad with a sherry dressing. For main: hake steak baked with an onion and lemon-rind confit, new potatoes with mint, green beans with tomatoes, garlic and basil. To finish: a chocolate soufflé with raspberries on the side, a shortbread biscuit, followed by a small whisky. Make that a double. Make it 73.32, The Scots Malt Whisky Society. Even though I don't live in Scotland any more, I wouldn't drink anything but Scottish whisky. Good malt is allowed for dessert. I say so, and it's my rules. This is me here doing this right now. I'm methodical. I tidy as I go along. They'd be proud, but the hell with them. My presentation is a sensation, back of the net! and the idiots have missed it. Their loss! Everything is delicious. *That is one plate of food, that is one plate of food.* That fish is cooked to *perfection. Perfect. Lovely, elegant dish. Well done! Phwoar! Phwoar! That is outstanding! The girl can cook. Well done!* I put the fish skin in the bin, and start on the chocolate soufflé, rich, velvety, darkly enigmatic chocolate soufflé, seriously tart raspberries. *Charming, absolutely delightful.* I knock back the whisky. *That is one cheeky wee whisky, inspired, absolutely, inspired and inspiring. Now that, that is almost alchemy! I mean like, wow!*

I'm losing weight, and it's a consolation. Bye-bye, junk food, cheerio, Big Mac! So long, French fries. It is falling off me. I don't need to lie to the scales any more. I can sing to the scales instead. But something's missing. I'm not a complete success story. Maybe because the dog's diet has been a disaster and the dog is still fat? Or maybe, it'd be nice to have someone to cook for. My old friend Ali, what would she like to eat now? Maybe she'd prefer fish and chips to red mullet with lemon and bay? Maybe she'd love sea bream stuffed with fennel? I'm not sure. We were nineteen before we saw a corn on the cob. I was twenty-two before I tasted avocado. Didn't think much of it in the beginning, but that was because I tried to eat the skin as well. Then I had a terrible time with an artichoke, not a Jerusalem artichoke but the kind that has a heart. I ate the heart but I ate the hair round the heart too, and coughed for a week.

Maybe I could cook Ali my special Arabic chicken with pine nuts and saffron with a lemon pilaf and a green salad? I'd make sure I didn't burn the pine nuts this time. What else? I can't think. I can't think of anything. I'm tired out thinking about what to eat. It's exhausting. What a holiday! I'd have been better off trailing around the Vatican. At least I might have got to see the Pope.

Next week I must go back to work and face the music. I don't really like my work colleagues. They moan all the time, and they are intensely competitive. It is a whole culture of moaning. Anyway next week, holiday over, back to face the music. Do you want to know where that expression comes from? Someone sits and stares at the radio; someone else won't take their eyes off the hi-fi; someone fixates on their piano until, what, until the music starts, and it lifts you, and lifts you some more, until finally you are not in your life at all, you're in another life entirely. That's what's going to happen to me when I face the music. It's going to be so different, so very, very fine. That is really going to happen to me. I'm like, can't wait.

These are not my clothes

These are not my clothes, I tell her. These are not my clothes, but she puts them on me anyway. She says lift your arms – that's it, over your head, there now, all fresh, as if I were a bloody baby. Everything belongs to everybody here, she says, what's it matter? These are not my clothes, I repeat. I heard you the first time, she says.

Then she takes me to the window, and parks me, bit of a wind today, she says, a good drying day. I sit and look out. What I see are the trees waving as if they are asking for help, or as if they are saying we surrender. There is an empty wooden table in the garden with a red umbrella down and not up in the middle because there is no sunshine. And there is a blue pot with some flowers I used to know the name of, but I have forgotten, so I'll call them forgotten flowers. There are forgotten flowers in the blue pot. And a bench – nobody is sitting on it; the bench is staring straight ahead as if it is watching something, maybe a match. There is a huge high hedge I think or it could be a stone wall with things growing through it. It is difficult to decipher things; where things begin to grow. Further ahead, I see white and purple and yellow small flowers with a very common name which I've just remembered: crocuses. Crocuses, crocuses! Round the crocuses is a small wall, a brick high. In the middle of the long lawn and not far from the table there is an apple tree, I think, but no apples and no apple blossom.

At the bottom of the long garden and through the trees, I can see another house in the distance, faintly, just a little red brick through the trees. And over to my left, and above the high hedge, I can see a slate roof and a cream chimney; and if I try to turn and peer round the corner, more to my left, moving slightly out of my chair, I can see the tree that cries, the one we used to call the weeping willow. I can see a bit of the weeping willow, not all of it because I can't crane round far enough. And that is my view from the window.

Yesterday, when she got me from this same place at the window, she said, you're lucky; we've got nice views here. I don't have my watch any more because they've taken it. At lunch, the other day, I saw Hannah wearing my watch, and when I said, Hannah I think someone's given you my watch, Hannah said very crossly, This is my watch. I went to argue with her and then felt as if something was clapping my mouth shut with such force that I didn't speak at all for the rest of the day. Life is too short to argue about time. I stared at my watch on Hannah's arm. Her arm had quite a few bumps on it and a lot of bruising, blue and black bruising. She looked a mess and her hair hadn't been brushed properly in a long time. She bent to her bowl of soup and ate the soup with a lot of slurping and dribbling. Her nails needed cutting, I noticed, as she brought the spoon to her mouth with my watch on her wrist.

Today, she comes for me and I assume it must be the same time as yesterday when she came for me. Worked up an appetite, have you? she asks me. I hope you're not going to be wasting your food today, are you? Think of the children in the famine. When she speaks, she speaks slowly and half-shouts, clearly enunciating her words, as if I were a dummy. She pushes me to the big oval table where all the women and the men are seated already, and she ties a bib round my neck to protect the blouse and cardigan that are not my clothes. These are not my clothes, I say to her again, and she says, Change the record, change the record, why don't you? And she pinches my arm quite hard. The soup is red and the spoon next to the soup is round. The spoon is not square because you couldn't fit a square spoon into a round mouth. The soup is red because it couldn't be blue. But yesterday it was yellow, you can get yellow soup and green soup, you know, but you can't really get black or blue soup. Unless you had a soup made of squid ink, but I doubt that would be very nice.

The matron in her blue and white uniform, mainly white, but with a blue and white stripe near her wide neck, says Grace and we must all hang our heads. For some of us the hanging of heads is the usual position anyway and there's no effort at all involved in Grace.

For what we are about to eat, may the Lord make us truly thankful, the matron says in a crisp voice, as crisp as that lettuce whose name I've forgotten. The matron then raises her head and looks over at me. She can tell I haven't hung my head and am looking straight ahead. Amen, she says, and stares at me. Of course I know that the matron wants me dead. Amen, I say and stare back at her. It's my face she always looks at when she says Amen.

I lift the spoon to my mouth and then put it back to the bowl; I lift it again and put it back to the bowl. I move the soup around the plate so that it looks disturbed; it looks like somebody has done something with it, so that the Matron will not notice that it is undisturbed. None of us talks to each other because nobody now has anything to say. It seems they have taken all the conversation from us. Sometimes, when someone is new here, they will make a bit of an effort and say something like, 'I used to enjoy watching the snooker, you know,' or 'I used to write to my daughter in Ontario once a month,' or 'I used to be very good at making shortcrust pastry,' or 'I used to go to the baths once a week on a Thursday while my wife was at the hairdresser's.' Or 'I was very involved in politics, you know.' Sometimes the new arrival will say something like that as if trying to remember who you once were helped. But what I've discovered is that it doesn't help what you used to do, or who you used to be. It doesn't help one jot. Not one jot.

There now, she says, back to your lovely view, don't you thank God that you're not staring at a brick wall? she says. And she parks me up. I can see the red umbrella which is still down because the sun still isn't shining, waving in the wind, and the leaves fluttering like lifted skirts or butterflies. Even the crocuses, yes the crocuses, are nodding their tiny heads in the wind. The bench still has nobody sitting on it and has bowed its head too; it is staring at something I can't see, maybe a book. Maybe the bench is reading a book. Maybe the bench is reading *Madame Bovary* – that was the name of a book I once read, *Madame Bovary*. It was written by Flaubert. Maybe the bench is French. The trees are now waving with a great grand gesture, a little over the top surely, as if they were at a football match, and altogether performing a great stadium wave, out of desperation, perhaps nobody has scored in the longest time. The trees are Mexican-waving like an actual goal would be a complete impossibility; perhaps in the whole history of football nobody has actually scored a goal; perhaps Pele and Best never existed, the trees are saying. But strangely, the weeping willow that is just out of view is still, though it must be experiencing the same wind. Perhaps it is too far away for me to see it weeping.

She comes in a while and brings a cup of tea and a ginger snap. When she comes I tell her these are not my clothes, and she says, shut up about your bloody clothes. You're getting on my nerves now. You're like

a broken record. Your needle's stuck in the one groove!
She laughs to herself, as if she's surprised herself by
being clever. I shut my mouth tight again and feel the
roof of my mouth push down on my tongue until my
lips purse. I have money in my purse, I say. Can you
get my purse? I'll ask if I can have a new cardigan
bought. There's a nice girl that comes in once a week
with black skin and curly hair and the darkest eyes
you have ever seen. She would go out, I'm sure, if I
find my purse, and buy me my own new cardigan. I sip
at my tea and I nibble at my ginger snap. I don't dip
or plunge my ginger snap into my tea because I've
seen many others here do that and quite frankly, it is
expected of us. I will ask Vadnie to get me a cherry red
cardigan the colour of the soup today. I won't need to
explain to Vadnie; I won't need to say cardigans can
be the same colour as soup; she knows that's the kind
of complicated world we live in.

When she comes to collect my cup, she is surprised
to see I've drunk my tea and eaten my biscuit. Good for
you, she says, well done. I will put a gold star on the
board at the bottom of your bed, she says. Now, why
don't you have your forty winks, forty winks in front
of a window with a lovely view – *get you*! she says and
laughs. My taking the tea has obviously made her very
happy. Perhaps she thinks she's now winning the match
that the bench is watching. I smile up my sleeve because
she doesn't know about the cardigan. She doesn't know
I've got a game plan. Game on, I might say.

I wonder who first decided it should be forty winks, why not fifty or thirty? And why should we all agree that it is forty winks we take when we nap? I try not to take any winks because I don't trust them. I don't want to fall asleep in my chair and suddenly end up back in my bed till dinner time. That's what they do if you take forty winks, wheel you back and lift you onto the bed in the small room with no view. They can leave you there in the afternoon for three or four hours, I think. Of course I'm not certain because Hannah has my watch. The ludicrous thing about Hannah having my watch is that she can't tell the time, or if she can, she doesn't realize what the time means. I asked her the other day to prove a point. I said, Hannah, what time is it and Hannah stared at my watch for ages and suddenly shouted six o'clock when it couldn't possibly be six o'clock because we had just had lunch. Matron glared at me. Don't keep mithering Hannah about the time, she said, as if I were the one that was being cruel. You don't need to know the time, anyway. We know the time, and we're in charge of the time, the time is none of your business. She gave a little incredulous laugh. I looked around me when she said this, to see what the others made of it. I couldn't believe she had been so blatant, so unsubtle. But nobody registered anything on their faces. Their faces were like the empty bowls, lined and ridged with the remains of things.

The blue pot in the garden in front of the bench is what I would call an electric blue. The flowers inside it

are what I would call dusty pink. I still can't think of
their name but they might be peonies, though I don't
know if they pot peonies or not. The sky, I haven't
mentioned the sky today, have I, is light grey, the
colour of doves. She comes again and she says, having a
peaceful rest are we? She seems to think there's two of
me. It's the only thing I'd agree with her about because
there are two of me. There's the one that's sat on this
chair and there's the one that's planning the Cardigan.
She wouldn't think for a second that I was capable of
planning such an elaborate stunt, or of pulling it off.
Though once I get that cardigan on, I won't be pulling
it off. I will keep it on. I will sleep with it under my
pillow, my red cardigan, and in the morning I'll put it
over the someone else's blouse and as long as I can have
my very own cherry red cardigan, I won't mind if it is
pulled over the blouse. But it is going to be vital that
I don't only obtain my new cardigan but that I fight to
keep it once I have it. I will have to find hiding places.

These are not my clothes, I say to her in answer to
her question about whether or not I'm having a peaceful
rest. What is it with you? she says and she pulls my
hair very hard. I don't know. I try to be nice and you
just ruin it all the time. You make me do this time and
again. She pinches the skin on the back of my neck
really hard and yanks my hair again. Do you enjoy it?
Is that it? When she asks me that question her eyes
suddenly shine with excitement. Do you enjoy it? We
enjoying this, are we?

I keep my mouth clamped shut, clamped like a flower that won't open, when I look out at my view or like a car, clamped like a car parked on double yellow lines. The bruises can go from blue and black to yellow and a sort of green you know; they change like traffic lights. If you mix two primary colours, you get another colour. I used to know them all: blue and yellow makes green, and red and blue makes purple, but before you know it when you think of colours you are back to bruises. She has gone now and left me to look at the view. When Vadnie comes, I will take money from my purse and I'll tell her to tell NO ONE that she is buying me a red cardigan and to bring it in a nondescript bag.

She takes me to dinner; it must be six. She parks me up against the table. She has a look on her face I can't quite read; perhaps it is defiance, or maybe hatred, or maybe just insouciance. A bit like the expression the bench has on its face when it is not watching the match, waiting, just waiting. Perhaps she thinks I'm going to tell somebody. But then I look at the others round the table, many of us are colours we should not be: and as far as I know nobody has said anything. I'm certainly the one who she should most fear because I'm the one who still has my marbles. My marbles are many-coloured, like great and glorious eyes. I didn't like it when you had to give away your marbles when an opponent hit them, and I don't think I liked putting my marble in the big circle either but of course I can't vouch for that because I can't remember the kind of child I was, or indeed, if I ever was a child. There is a good chance that I never was a child. There's a high chance that I never had a past at all. Before she brought me to dinner, the bench had finished reading *Madame Bovary* and had started reading *A High Wind in Jamaica*. The bench, because it was windy, decided it wanted to read things with *wind* in the title but the bench was too old and too sophisticated for *Wind in the Willows* and, and the bench looked up its wooden nose at *Gone With The Wind*.

The nurse brings me to the table; she and the matron exchange a look. I think there are tears in my eyes, and that they are running down my face, though I would not want or wish them there. The matron comes up and whispers, Go Easy or you'll get us into trouble. It chills me. I know now for certain that the nurse and the matron are in cahoots with each other. I used to simply think that the matron was cruel because she gave me those looks at Grace, but now I know she knows it is a whole different game of marbles. I might have to ask Vadnie to also get me a pair of slacks. A pair of navy blue slacks. If I were dressed head to toe in my own clothes, I might have a chance of getting out of here. Vadnie might not know that slacks means trousers, any person under fifty might not know that, just like they might not know what a kimono is or a caftan or a twinset or a rain hat, or even a sou'wester

or a flapper dress. Mind you, they all know about
ponchos these days. I was surprised when my son last
brought my granddaughter, Abbie, that she was wearing a poncho. So . . . I might have to say, Vadnie, with
the money from my purse, could you also buy me a pair
of navy blue casual trousers size ten? The matron says,
For what we are about to receive will the Lord make us
truly thankful, and when she lifts her head she looks
over at me right away to see if I have bowed my head.
I have cried, that is probably evident, but I will not
bow my head. This time, the matron smiles at me. She
does not scowl. She smiles. I wouldn't say that it is a
sarcastic smile, or a nasty smile or even a false smile. It
looks to me as if the matron has just smiled a genuine
smile. I can't think what will be happening to me next.

The dinner is stew, beef stew, I think, but it might
be lamb, some kind of meat anyway with little diced
carrots in it, and potatoes. The matron eats her food
with the confidence of someone who has lovely things
from the delicatessen saved in her locker. There are
little bits of gristle on the meat and tiny lumps of
undisclosed jelly in the gravy. Some people are eating.
The matron is still looking at me and still smiling. You
know that if you don't eat your food at the table, you'll
have to be transferred, she says. You know what that
means, don't you? I pick up my fork and shovel some
of the ghastly gristle into my mouth. I don't want to
be transferred; if I am I won't see Vadnie and I won't

be able to get my cardigan. All of these places are as bad as each other. Vadnie is what makes this place bearable, just.

After dinner, I'm parked in front of the television. Peggy is asked what she would like to watch because Peggy always says I don't mind and then the matron says, well let me choose for you and so we all watch Matron's programmes. Anything after nine that involves a killing, that's for me, Matron always announces proudly, as if she possessed a particular talent for self-knowledge. Who do you think did it, Margaret? Matron always asks me, because she knows I'm the only one in this place that can work things out, who still has her marbles. Too many red herrings, I say and nod meaningfully. A red herring, dried, smoked and salted, drawn across a fox's path, destroys the scent and faults the hounds, I say, suddenly remembering a piece of knowledge. Ssssh, says Matron irritably. It's a long time since I had a piece of herring, a long time since I had any fish at all. I try and think of names of fish whilst watching *Morse* to amuse myself: cod, haddock, hake, salmon, tuna, mackerel, herring, plaice, sole, what's the one that they cook the tail . . . monkfish, mullet, John Dory. Its name was doré the French for golden long before the John came along. It has an oval black spot on each side said to be the finger marks of St Peter when he held the fish to extract the coin. Isn't the Bible fascinating, I say to no one in particular as Morse plays a piece of Chopin. At least I think it is Chopin.

Hannah, sitting next to me with my watch on, says six o'clock! Shut up with your six o'clock, the nurse says to Hannah. Six o'clock, shouts Hannah like she's choosing to be a parrot for the day. Do you want to be transferred, Hannah? the nurse says. Is that what you want? Six o'clock, Hannah says again and the nurse almost runs at her. Careful! says the matron, pressing pause on the remote control. The nurse wheels Hannah out of the television room and away. (That was the last time I ever saw Hannah.) When the programme finishes and the killer is uncovered, Matron switches off the main light and leaves on just the side lights. Who is for bed? she asks almost pleasantly.

Quite a few of us put up our hands. We are all for bed really. We will all be for bed all the time eventually. Soon enough, if we are not sorry, none of us will even have our special view at the window. Every day I take in as much of it as possible. She parks me and lifts me off the chair and onto my bed. I have not been changed today and these are not my clothes, I say. The nurse pulls out the sodden pad from inside my paper pants and chucks it into the waste bin. Somebody's been busy today, she says, and shoves another pad into me. At least I've got a fresh pad to go to sleep in, I must be thankful for small mercies. Sometimes, she deliberately sends me to sleep with the one I've had in all day and when she comes next morning she says, Oh dear – did I forget to change you last night? There are sores on my legs, not a pretty sight. Painful too, but

I try and ignore the pain of things, especially if I am at the window. I am given my pills, I swallow them, bitter red and yellow and white and pink pills, and lie on my pillow which is not fresh, not as fresh as my pad, and try and count sheep. I lie wondering why it was sheep they told us to count, whoever it was who chose that first, and why not cows, or goats or donkeys or dogs or pigs or horses or geese or llamas . . . why not llamas? And then I must have fallen off.

I dream I am a young woman again wearing a pleated skirt and a red cardigan, and my hair is long and thick and brown and stretches all the way down my back, so long I could sit on my hair if I wanted to. In my dream I'm amazed that my hair could ever be so long. Even in my dream, I must somehow realize that I am now an old woman with cropped grey hair.

In the morning, Vadnie is there, smiling. She has a wide and lovely smile. How are you, Margaret? Vadnie! I say struggling up on the bed as she brings me my cup of tea and my bowl of porridge. We never eat breakfast in the dining room – only lunch and dinner. Vadnie! I say urgently. We don't have much time. Would you be able to find my purse? It is right at the back of my locker underneath my toilet bag? The last time my son came to visit I told him to put it there. Vadnie looks at me a little sadly. It's not there, she says, Don't you remember we looked for it last week? Well, it has to be somewhere, I say, a little crossly. Look again. Vadnie bends down and opens the locker. It is not this, she says, holding up my toilet bag, and not this, she says, holding up a letter, and not this, holding a magazine my son bought me. What is it you want to buy? Vadnie asks me. Tell me. Maybe I can help? I want to buy a red cardigan, I say, and a pair of slacks. A pair of what? Vadnie says. A casual pair of trousers, size ten, in navy, I say. And I don't want anybody else to wear them, I want them hidden in my locker so they don't get taken away and when they need washing I only want you to do it because you are the only one in this building I trust. Vadnie smiles as if I've told her this before. I will get what you want and when you find your purse you can pay me back, she says. When my son comes, he'll give you the money, even if I don't ever find my purse. I think Nurse has stolen my purse, I whisper to Vadnie. Vadnie looks to the door, alarmed, sssshhhh, she says, though I can tell she doesn't doubt me. She knows what the pair of them is like. She's got the measure of Matron and Nurse.

After breakfast, Vadnie wheels me to my view, my, my, she says, it is windy today and no mistake and look how the rain is falling. The tallest tree on the east is waving right over to the west, I say to Vadnie and she nods. And look how the blossom is on that lovely tree at the bottom, she says pointing, and I gasp. I cannot believe I have missed the blossom, sitting here as I do day after day. Somehow I was concentrating on look-ing beyond to the space in the hedge where I can see the red brick and I just missed out the blossom. Isn't it sort of delicate like? Vadnie says, smiling. It's like you, Margaret, frail and beautiful. It's like lace. Here, who are you calling frail? I say to Vadnie jokingly, and laugh a little because I feel not only is Vadnie back, but I'm back. She is the only one in this place who really knows me. This godforsaken place, I should say. But I don't because today is a Vadnie day and so it doesn't feel godforsaken. It feels blessed, blessed as blossom. Once, long ago, when I gave birth to my son, the midwife was called Blossom, I tell Vadnie. You remind me a little of Blossom. One of your daughters is called Ladyblossom if I remember right? That's right, Vadnie says. I kind of liked that name. Where was she from, Blossom? Vadnie asks me, and I surprise myself because I've remembered the answer: Barbuda, I say. Blossom was from Barbuda. That so, Vadnie says. And then she says, I'll leave you to your view, don't forget to look at that blossom now and I'll try and get your red cardigan and what do you call them, slacks?, in my lunch time and if not then, then I'll bring them next time OK? Sure now? OK?

She's holding my hand and patting it softly. It is only when she is here that you remember what it is like to be touched in a nice way. I pat the back of her hand too. OK, I say, OK. I firmly believe she will be back with my red cardigan and my navy slacks tomorrow. I don't remember being as excited about anything in a long, long time. The rain isn't falling in a straight line. It is falling in slants and it's almost hard to see that it is actually raining. You have to stare out the window very hard to see the movement of the rain. If you look near the ground you see it, the sky's great tears. It might be miserable out there; but inside my head it's not raining, not raining like it is on the empty table and chairs with the red umbrella that is still not up, though they could put it up to keep the table dry if they wanted to, and not raining like it is on the bench which is not watching the match any more because it has been called off because of the rain, so the bench has nothing to do except face the weeping willow and weep. The grass however is really benefiting from the rain and is a deeper green than before. The grass *is* actually greener on the other side. I'd like to share this joke with somebody, but there is nobody to share it with. Iris has fallen asleep deep into her chest at the viewpoint next to me and Harry too is asleep with his head back and his mouth open. I'm awake watching the green grass, the green green grass of home. Who was it who sang that again? Him with the handsome face and the funny name? Was it Engelbert Humperdinck? No, no it wasn't. It was Tom Jones. He hasn't got a funny name. His name is quite ordinary, though he does have a handsome face. So did Humperdinck have a handsome face. What was his song? Release me (And let me love once again!). Nurse arrives to take me to lunch. And how are we today? she asks of the two of us, the me who is here and the me who is not here. We are fine, I say and Nurse looks like you could have knocked her over with a feather. Oh yes, we are fine and dandy, we are quite spiffing! I say just so she can be sure she heard right. Well, this makes a change! Nurse says. No whingeing today, eh? She tugs my hair. No crying, no complaining? Nope, I say, moving my head elegantly out of her way and shaking it, proudly tilting my chin, so that it is up in the air and my head is a little back, No, certainly not. We are fine today because our lawyer is arriving at noon. Come again? says the nurse, looking, I must say a little apprehensive. You heard the first time, I say, using my deep voice. You better get a smart suit, lady, because you are going to court!

Matron says Grace, for what we are about to receive malarkey again. I feel slightly giddy, as high as a kite, as if somebody had just given me a small glass of bubbly. I know I've put the wind up the nurse, that's for sure. I lift the spoon to my mouth. It is tomato soup again. Cherry red tomato soup, the same colour as the cardigan that Vadnie is going to be bringing me tomorrow. This soup is actually very woolly, I say and Matron looks at me in a calculated fashion, as if she were trying to second-guess me. It is certainly true, that if people are your foes, it is best to keep them on their toes, I think to myself and want to share this joke too, but there is nobody around of the calibre to appreciate it. I will save it for Vadnie when she comes with my brand-new clothes. Or perhaps I will tell my son when he comes to visit with Abbie. But he, I know for sure, will look at me with pity and disdain, and say, Don't you get fed up talking in these silly riddles? and I'll say, My boy these riddles are saving my life, and he'll roll his eyes because he has no idea, he has absolutely no idea. None of them have. None of them have a single clue what this place is really like. Not a single clue. Not one iota. After lunch, I'm parked at my viewpoint.

It comes as a complete surprise, the little red robin that arrives from nowhere to sit on the bench and the black bird that comes to sit on the empty table under the red umbrella. I'm breathless with excitement. And almost exactly at the same time, a thrush flies over the hedge and into the garden of the house next door where I understand a family live. It was quite something to see how it swooped and curled in the air before heading there. The three birds reminded me that I, when I first came to sit here, used to hear the bird song and I couldn't remember if the sound I was hearing was the song of the blackbird or the thrush. But I took it as communication anyway. I imagined those birds looking in at me with their beady, birdy eyes, looking in at me looking out at them. I imagined, like the birds in a children's fairy tale, the gallant birds leading me to safety. Today it is not the word wind I will use for my viewpoint game, or fish, but bird. And not books, but songs. Pack up all your . . . how does it go again . . . something and woe, here we go, to and fro, Bye Bye blackbird. Is it that? Is it something like that? Yes, wait a minute, Margaret. *Pack up all my care and woe /*

37

here I go / Singing low / Bye Bye Blackbird / where somebody waits for me / Sugar's sweet so is she / Bye Bye Blackbird. Something like that.

Nurse comes and says abruptly, is that you singing to yourself, Margaret? And I say, yes, that's me singing to myself. By the way, she says smiling. Vadnie won't be coming in today. She waits for me to say something. I thought I'd better tell you. We had to let her go. We found out she was stealing from people. The bench can't think of any more songs with birds in it. Not a single song. What does the bench look like under the moonlight. Moon. Songs with the word moon. Why can't the bench think of things any more? 'She won't be coming back,' Nurse is saying to me. Who, I say to her, who won't be coming back?

The First Lady of Song

My father wasn't thinking of me when he kept me alive for years. I was my father's experiment. At the end of this long life, when my skin is starting to show its age, finally, and my hair has the shy beginnings of grey, I need to speak. I've got out of the way of talking. It's so much easier to sing, *Da dee dee dee di deeeee.* Talking, I always trip myself up, make some nasty mistake. It's had the effect of people thinking of me as crazy, *doo–lah–li–lal.* I've learnt to talk lightly about things, just skimming the surface, in case I found myself in trouble. It is difficult to know where to begin – *doh ray me fah so lah ti doh* – for me there was no real beginning. I knew nothing of what was happening to me. One day, I was my old self, those years ago, carefree, spontaneous, and loving; another day, those qualities had gone. When I was first drugged, I fell into a coma, apparently. I was in that coma for a week; my father told me when I came round. He seemed delighted about my coma, he smiled, patted my head, and said, 'I think it's worked; it's a miracle.' I fled. I left my father, my mother, my sisters and brothers. I never looked back, and he never found me. Back in those early days, I had a different name. My name was Elina Makropulos. I've had many husbands, countless children, grandchildren, great-grandchildren. Some of my children are a blur, but the pianos are vivid – the babies and the uprights, the ebony and ivory, the little Joes.

I remember time through music – what I was singing when. How I loved those Moravian folk songs, how I lost myself in those twelve-bar blues, how I felt understood by those soaring arias, how beautiful ballads kept me company, how scatting made me feel high. For years I've been singing my head off, singing my head off for years. When I sang Elina's head off, Eugenia came. When I sang Eugenia's head off, Ekateriana came. When I sang Ekateriana's arias, Elisabeth came. After Elisabeth I was Ella. My favourite period was my Ella period. Every song I sang had my own private meanings: 'I Didn't Mean A Word I Said', 'Into Each Life Some Rain Must Fall', 'Until The Real Thing Comes Along', and even 'Paper Moon'. I'd lived so long, nothing was real. Ella seemed to be cool about that. *Bebop, doowop! Eeeeee deee dee dee dee de ooooooooooh dahdada-dada bepop doowop brump bum bump.*

Now, I'm Emilia Marty. I'm in the middle of being Emilia Marty. I've returned to being a classical singer, my first love. My voice is deeper now. I've sung about every type of love through all the years. Back when I was Elina Makropulos, my skin was pale, perhaps a little translucent. As the years went on, I got darker

and darker. Now, my skin is dark black. Emilia Marty
has dark black skin. I'm rather in awe of it. It is not
transparent, it is not translucent, but it is shimmering.
I wear a great dark skin now, like a dark lake, like a
lake at night with a full moon in the sky. Way back in
the days when my father first drugged me, I remember
seeing the last moon I ever saw as Elina Makropulos;
the last moon before I fell into a coma. It was a new
baby moon, rocking in its little hammock, soft-skinned,
fresh. Or it was the paw of a baby polar-bear cub,
clawing at the sky. Or it was a silver fish leaping
through the deep, dark sea-sky. That's the only other
thing that's accompanied me on my long journey, the
moon. The moon has never been boring! I wrote a
song for it back in my Ella days: *Blue Moon, I saw you
standing alone.*

I've been lonely with my lies for years. I told none
of my many children the truth about their mother. I
didn't want them to carry the burden. I wanted them
to think that they had an ordinary mother who looked
good for her years, who was pretty healthy perhaps.
Every time I ran into an old friend or acquaintance
who said, 'It's remarkable, you haven't changed a bit,'
I smiled grimly and knew that they were telling the
absolute truth. None of them knew that it was the
truth, or how uncanny their little clichés were for me.
'You don't look a day older than the last time I saw
you,' 'Your skin hasn't got a single line,' these were

sickening sentences for me. The only change for me was my skin gradually darkening, yet nobody noticed this. Nobody lived long enough!

I'd sing my children lullabies, and chortle to myself when I got to *Your daddy's rich and your ma is good-looking* knowing full well that daddy would die first and so would baby, and that the person who should really want to cry was me – *Hush Hush, little baby.* When nobody knows who you truly are, what's the point in living? We're not alive to be alone on the planet. We're alive to share, to eat together and love together and laugh together and cry together. If you can never love because you will always lose, what reason is there to live? I have lost husbands, daughters, and sons. When my father used me as his experiment I don't imagine he ever thought properly about the life of grief he was consigning me to, the grief, handed down the long line of years, a softening grey bundle of it. After a while, I stopped loving anyone so that I wouldn't be hurt by their death. If you are certainly going to outlive all your family and your friends, who keeps you company? Only the songs knew me – only the songs – the daylight and the dark, the night and the day. Perhaps he might have thought of it as a gift. There is no way for me to go back and unpick the years to find out what my father hoped for me. The truth is more uncomfortable, I think. He didn't consider me in the equation. I was his experiment. He didn't know if it would work or not. Even now, all this time away, I can't stop myself from wondering. I cannot fathom my father.

I have not loved for so many years, I can't really be sure of how it feels, if it is good or if it is frightening. If it is deep, how deep it goes, to which parts of the body and the mind? I have no real idea. My biggest achievement was getting rid of it altogether. What a relief! I remember that. The sensation of it! The day that I discovered I could no longer love. It was like a lovely breeze on a hot day. It billowed and felt really quite fine. I remember when, some time ago, I stood, a young woman at the grave of my old son, and not a tear came. I said to myself, 'He was tone deaf that one, he could never sing,' and laughed later that night, drinking a big goblet of wine. Years later, I remember being at the funeral of my old daughter, a vicious tongue she had, that one, I said to myself and threw the rose in. *So, goodbye, dear.* I tried to remember if I had ever taken pleasure in any of her childhood, in reading her a book, or holding her small hand, or buying her a wooden doll. And though I had done those things, I think, I could not remember getting any pleasure. I could not remember getting anything at all.

People would say that I was the world's greatest singer, back when I was Ella, I had a vocal range spanning three octaves and a pure tone, my dear. They said on the one hand I seemed to feel and know everything and on the other, I had never grown up.

(True, true!) I could sing the greatest love songs and yet appear as if nothing touched me, as if I'd never had sex. Nobody but myself knew the irony in the way I sang Gershwin's, *The way you wear your hat, the way you sip your tea, the memory of all that, no, no they can't take that away from me.* I sang it defiantly, despite the fact that they were taking it away from me all the time, and one husband's hat frankly had blended into another's and I barely noticed the way they sipped their tea, let alone remembered it. When I sang Cole Porter's *I've got you under my skin, so deep in the heart of me, so deep in my heart that you're really a part of me*, I was singing to myself, to Elina, Eugenia, Ekateriana, Elisabeth, I was trying to keep myself together.

I had sex over and over again. Sometimes I'd get lost in it; sometimes it was the only thing that could go right through me, where I could banish the lonely feeling and abandon myself to somebody else, the soft skin of an earlobe, anybody's earlobe, the smell of morning breath, the hair on a chest. For a moment, any little intimacy would make me feel I was standing on a smallholding, and not out in the vast, yellow, empty plains, the wind roaring on my face, singing my plain-song. I barely remember some of my men; the love songs lasted way longer than the lovers. Some were large and some were small, but all seemed to be fertile, alas. And when child came out after child, between my legs and over the centuries, I would gaze down in a sort of trance, a huge boredom coming over me already, before the new baby even suckled on my breast. Another baby! So what! Another baby to feed and teach to read and count and watch die. I lost my children to typhus, whooping cough, scarlet fever, tuberculosis, cholera, small pox, influenza. Many of my children died before they were ten or fifteen. I remember a couple of hundred years ago looking wistfully at my daughter Emily, and wishing on the bone of the hard white moon that I could catch her whooping cough and die, die, die. It was never for me, death, never going to be handed out to me on a lovely silver platter, not the gurgle or the snap or the thud or the whack or the slide of it, death. No. I was consigned to listening to the peal of church bells barely change over the stretch of years.

When I came to be Ella, I was so much more independent. Those were plucky, scatting days. Even the moon bopped in the sky. I was on the road forty out of forty-five weeks. I'd come a long way. I'd gone from working with dodgy numbers runners to being the first African-American to perform at the Mocambo! Life takes odd turns. In my case, *lives* take odd turns. There I was finally as integrated as Elvis, singing songs by Jewish lyricists to white America, having folk like Marilyn Monroe fight in my corner. *Every time I say goodbye I cry a little*, I was saying goodbye all my life, I was saying goodbye to my other selves, Elina, Eugenia, Ekateriana, Elisabeth, Ella. My own names were a kind of litany. *When you're near I want to die a little*. Only the songs knew my secrets. When I was Elisabeth, I was known for how I sang Strauss's *Four Last Songs*. One time, late in my Elisabeth day, I was performing at the Albert Hall, singing Straussy for the umpteenth time, and I got to the last stanza. I felt like him; I welcomed death. I sang with true feeling – *O vast tranquil peace, so deep at sunset, how weary we are of wandering, is this perhaps death?* One of the reviewers said I'd grown into the songs over the years. Well, yes.

There's been so much to grow into over the years. I'm like an old person the way I pick out memories and cluck over them. Well, they say the old repeat them-selves and the young have nothing to say. The boredom is mutual! I've got an old woman's head in a young woman's body. *Thank you for the memories!* I remember: my excitement when I first got to fly on an aeroplane, getting adjusted to the phone and its ring, having penicillin suddenly for my children, my first X-ray, how my hair felt the first time it was blow-dried, how exciting, the indoor bath with running water, how bamboozling the supermarket was at first. There was nobody around who'd lived as long as me, nobody to say, I liked it before we had supermarkets, I liked it before zoos arrived, before we had aeroplanes, before the hole in the ozone, I liked living before all those things. I didn't like the poverty, the sickness, but there is still something to be said for a good cobbler, an honest loaf of bread, a cobbled street, bare oak beams, revolution. Even the words have kept changing over the centuries.

I've had to keep up with the Vocab. *Jeepers Creepers*. I've had to keep changing my talk. Bloggers. Tweeters. Finders keepers losers seekers. I've lived long enough to see *bourgeois* go out and *bespoke* come in, to see daguerrotype vanish and Facebook appear.

I took a boat trip down the Vltava River in Prague, many moons ago. The food in Prague – how I loved breast of duck with saffron apples, how I loved my mother's flaky apple strudel. I remember the first time I ate a sandwich in England and even when the word sandwich came in. My favourite pie ever was way back in the nineteenth century. They don't make them like that these days! It was filled with chicken, partridge and duck and had a layer of green pistachios in the middle. I don't remember who I was then, but I remember that pie! I remember when tea and coffee and sugar started being so popular. I remember my first drink of aerated water, ginger ale. I used to have a lovely silver spirit kettle. I remember the excitement of my first flask, how I took it on a lavish picnic. All musicians love a picnic. There's always been music and wine, concerts and hot puddings, strawberries, champagne. Food and claret and ale all seemed to taste better a while back. As I've gone through times, I've noticed so much getting watered down. Not just taste, but ideas. Oh for the fervour and passion of Marx now. Oh for the precociousness of Pascal. Oh the originality of Picasso.

My body never changed shape or height, give or take an inch or so. It was my colour that changed, and with my colour my voice. I've returned to singing the spirituals that I sang back in the days when I was another self. *Swing low, sweet chariot, coming forth to carry me home, swing low, sweet chariot, coming forth to carry me home. There is a balm in Gilead to make the wounded whole. There is a balm in Gilead to heal the sin-sick soul.* My voice is deeper than I could have ever believed when I was a soprano; if it was a colour it would be maroon. I go low, *Go down, Moses,* till my voice is at the bottom of the river bed, with the river reeds and marshes.

I look at myself in the mirror. My skin is still young-looking, and a dark blue-black colour. I look about thirty when I'm really three hundred years old. I've looked about thirty all these years. These days, it's easier for me to make up my face, to add a little lipstick, a little blusher, and mascara for my already very long eyelashes. My eyelashes have grown over the centuries and are now a lavish length. People comment on them. 'I've never seen such long eyelashes,' they'll say and I roll my eyes. I've been here a long time. There is nothing new under the sun, nothing that anyone can say. I've lost the ability to be surprised. Nothing about myself interests me. I've lost all vanity. I've lost my passion for ideas. I've lost my love of listening to the way that people talk, because I've found, over the years, people say more or less the same thing, and expect me to be riveted – the price of food, the price of fuel, the children, the schooling, the illness, the betrayal, the blow, the shock. Specific times and events jump out at me – I remember when the abolition of the slave trade was announced; when women first got the vote; when Kennedy was assassinated, when segregation and Jim Crow laws started to change. Actually, I really thought something might change properly in the nineteen-sixties. That was the last time I felt optimistic. I've lived through so much hurt, so many wars, so much hunger, so much unkindness and cruelty. At last, it seemed to me a decade when people cared, and the talk was interesting and I buzzed and sang and actually made some friends. And the friends I made seemed to care about me, and we all had pretty good sex with each other, sometimes three or four of us at the same time. It was liberating until it became narrow and selfish, and petty jealousies and concern about money started creeping in, and all those lovely sixties flower folk seemed to wake up and say, I want I want I want. And off they went, the marchers, protesters, petitioners, to see acupuncturists, therapists, homeopaths. So I crept off, changing my name again and my skin darkened. I bumped into one of my old friends twenty or so years later – I lose all track of time – and she had a bungalow, three kids, a garage, a drinks cabinet, a mortgage, a pension, a car and a broken heart. Her husband had gone running off with someone half her age. She looked at me wistfully and said, 'Oh but Emmy you haven't aged at all. It's quite incredible. You look exactly the same as the day I last saw you.' She stared at me, and looked worried. She was the first person that ever really knew in her bones that something was not right with me.

She invited me round to her house a few weeks later. 'What have you been doing, Emmy, did you get married, have children?' she said. I laughed, and told her the truth. I thought what have I got to lose? 'I've been alive for three hundred years,' I said, and she exploded laughing. 'Emmy,' she snorted, 'you always were so droll!' 'Children?' I laughed, 'I've had children, many, many children, and outlived the lot of them. 'Husbands?' I've had husbands over the centuries, and buried them all.' The tears were pouring down my innocent friend's face by now. 'What have I been doing?' I asked her back. 'I've seen kings and queens come and go. I've seen governments rise and fall. I used to have sympathy for the Whigs. I've lived in Czechoslovakia, America, England.' My friend's eyes glazed over. Suddenly, I wasn't funny, I was boring. She yawned. 'You're tired?' I asked, gathering speed. 'I'm exhausted. Imagine how tired you would be if you were three hundred years old?' 'Would you like a big gin?' she asked eagerly, desperate to change the subject. 'Yes,' I said, 'why the hell not after all the things I've seen. What about you?' I asked. The rest of the evening was spent on the husband, the betrayal, the younger woman that did not have a brain in her head, was skinny, was his secretary, how she'd not suspected a thing until . . . how, how, how. I felt myself droop into my gin. I squeezed her hand and noticed that she'd got drunk incredibly quickly. (That was something that didn't happen to me, incidentally. I'd learnt to watch the goblets over the years, to hold my drink.) She leaned towards me half-sozzled, her eyes a little vacant, a little dear departed, and she kissed me, or rather her lips slid across my mouth like a small child sliding down a shoot. I kissed her back and fondled a little at her breasts and then I left, opening and closing the door of the quietly disturbed bungalow.

With such a long life as mine, it's impossible to capture it. And maybe it is of no consequence. I don't know what I've learned that is all that different from anybody here for a shorter time. I think because I've never had to get on a bus with a walking stick, never had to think about stairs, never had to buy hair dye, worry about brittle bones, never had false teeth, never drawn a pension, never been in an old people's home, never had dementia, angina, because I've never had wrinkles, bald patches, plastic hips or knees, that I have been deprived! I've never had that tender frailty I've seen in the old, that sudden lost old-girl, old-boy vulnerability, that anxiety the old have about travelling anywhere different, packing and unpacking cases. I've pooh-poohed all of that for centuries, jumping on and off boats, trains, planes. I suddenly wanted it. I wanted to become old. I wanted to know what it was like to have death ahead of you finally, that I could let go, that my hair would go grey and curly. I longed for the simple business of getting old, giving myself a break, not singing for the world any more, not up on the big stages, staying in the big hotels, singing my heartless heart out.

Enough is enough is enough! I went back to Prague. I hadn't been there for years and could barely credit the change in my old town. Part of it had changed into Clubland! I traipsed round the old part of the city looking for the lawyer's office, through the Staromestke namesti, the old Town Square where I stood remembering my girlhood when the astronomical clock struck twelve and one hand rang a bell and a second overturned an hourglass. I'd forgotten the clock! How had I forgotten the astronomical clock? I wandered through the square in a daze, remembering how my father had told me about the twenty-seven people who were executed there. I walked on and on, through Wenceslas Square until finally I found it! The lawyer's office hadn't changed names. They hadn't moved buildings! I climbed the stairs with trepidation. I had no idea how long I was being consigned to live. In the office was a woman by the name of Kristina Kolenaty. She hunted for the precious document which revealed my father's secret. I paid her a handsome stack of euros and fled down the steps, down the street, back through the old square, down the achingly familiar street of alchemists, and back to my hotel. The document told me the details of the potion my father had given me, that would ensure I lived for ever, and the details of how to reverse it.

I didn't want to live for ever. I never did want to live for ever. There's no one to share your memories with except history books, and they get so much of it wrong. (Unbelievable, how much they distort and omit!) When I got the formula, I didn't even hesitate. I mixed the spoonfuls of X and X and Y and ZH together in the exact proportions and I threw it down my neck and I swallowed. I gulped emphatically, making a sound with it, a kind of animal sound. *Non, Je Ne Regrette Rien, Non, Rien De Rien*, I sang at the top of my voice. Then I lay down on the hotel-room bed, waiting for something to happen to me, listening out for it, as if I was listening for the sound of slippers walking along the corridor. I felt a little uncertain, a little frightened. Nothing happened. Nothing happened. I returned to my house in London and waited. I stopped singing publicly. I had no desire to be famous any more, no desire to sing to anybody but myself in the bath. I had plenty of money. I gave as much as I could away. Years passed, and still not a single sign – not a grey hair, nothing. My face was the same face in the mirror that it had been for centuries.

A few weeks ago, I was in the queue for the first day at the Proms. I got chatting to a lovely woman with a very beautiful face. She had curly hair. Dark winged eyebrows. I could see her hair was dyed. I liked that. She had a few, maybe one or two kind wrinkles around her eyes. She was large-ish, like me, a big bosom and belly. We talked about music we loved. Her eyes were shining. She had something about her that was quite, quite special. We'd been talking for ages before we found out each other's names. 'Irene,' she said. 'Emilia,' I said. 'I thought so,' she said. 'I thought it was you.' I was trying to work out her age; for the first time in my long life, I found myself interested in someone's age. 'What age are you if you don't mind me asking?' I asked her. 'Fifty-seven,' she said. 'Me too,' I said. I'd guessed I must be roughly that by now. We stood together, promming it. She'd brought along some champagne and some very delicious sandwiches. I felt comfortable in my skin. We stood listening, rapt and happy like two women that had known each other all of her life, if not all of mine! When the Prom finished, I could sense her sadness. 'Would you like to go out some time to a concert together or for a meal?' I asked her and her smile lit up her face, the river, the night sky. I could feel something quite extraordinary happening to me. I could feel myself soften and give in. My heart, something was happening to my heart that hadn't happened for years. I could hear it thrumming and strumming and chiming. I could feel my body trembling, vibrato style. I looked at her eyes, deep into her eyes, and I felt euphoric. It was a wonder. That night I found myself singing, *Good night, Irene, good night, Irene, I'll see you in my dreams*, before climbing into my double bed on my own. I slept, dreaming her. 'You are quite wonderful,' I told her on our sixth date. 'Oh,' she said, smiling, shy, 'you are not so bad yourself.'

That night I was putting my night cream on my face when I saw it. A little grey hair. I stared at it astonished. So frail, I might not have noticed it. How lovely! A few weeks later, another, and another. I looked again. 'Hello, little wrinkle,' I said gently. Well hello dolly! A while after that I got my first fuming red-hot flush. It wasn't so great, but I couldn't complain! I'm looking forward to getting past the flushes and into proper old age. I'm very much looking forward to it, creaking bones, memory lapses. What a lovely word – dotage! What jolly delightful words: old age.

Last night, I went to bed humming an old song I hadn't sung for years. It was like I'd written that verse waiting for her to come along, and then my own song suddenly made sense. I opened the curtains. A big wise moon glowed in the sky, the same moon that had been there since time. The moon appeared to me like a listening eye. I sang to it before I climbed into bed. I sang to the moon and I sang to Irene. For the first time in my long life, I really wanted to live. *You knew just what I was there for. You heard me saying a prayer for / Somebody I really could care for.*

The Pink House

I had a big wad of money once about twenty years ago. I blew the lot. If I hadn't blown the lot, I'd be dead by now. I needed to throw dosh around to stay alive. I could do with those readies now. I keep thinking if I had just put some of it away, I'd be sitting pretty. I've got debts that flutter in my head all night. When I tried to get an unsecured personal loan to pay off other loans, there were sharks' teeth marks against my name. I had to write to this place and pay two pounds to find out my credit history which wasn't pretty. It is scary that all that stuff is kept about you, marks against your name – blodges and splots and stains. Are you a person of integrity? No, you are a liability. Are you going up or are you going down? You're going down. Six missed Visa payments in a row. I'm not Elizabeth Ellen; I am a bad debt.

I have become very frightened of bills when they come in with their sharp beaks. What I do instead of opening them is not open them. I put them all in a pile and occasionally I stand against the pile and when it reaches my knee – I am not all that tall – I begin a new pile. I never risk the pile of post reaching my neck, though I do wake myself up at night in a clammy sweat, and say to myself in a very mean voice to stop myself from sleeping, 'You're in it up to your neck, up to your neck!' If I talk to myself harshly enough, I might win the lottery. There's got to be somebody watching out for me who knows I'm not taking it lightly, somebody who would give me a bloody break, a second chance. Somebody who knows I am ashamed to the core of my being.

I am starting to get persistent calls from one of my credit-card companies. *This call is for Elizabeth Ellen*, the voice says and then repeats *Elizabeth Ellen.* Hanging up's no good; it just rings back. *This call is for Elizabeth Ellen*. It drives me to the wall and back. I try and pay some interest off with another piece of plastic which also needs paying off. I find that if you rotate the cards, like people used to do with crops, you can get by for a bit longer. When the machine voice says, *please enter the long number at the front of your card*, I punch the numbers in. Of course, you are always having to prove who you are first. Post code, date of birth, mother's maiden name. The thing is I don't know who I am. All I know is that I am heavily pregnant and heavily in debt. And that I am peeing a shocking amount. And I am forty-one, what they call at the hospital an elderly primagravida. I don't like the sound of that. It makes me sound all used up already. Does life begin at forty for the elderly primagravida? I don't think so.

I was brought up to always pay back what I owed,

to not spend a penny more than I had. I was brought up with a piggy bank, for goodness' sake. I loved my little piggy bank. I knew how to save; I could budget. Then my life split open and saving was the thing that I lost. I couldn't save money any more; I was too busy saving my life. I knew how to spend. The more I spent, the more I needed to spend. I didn't just spend a penny. I spent pounds and pounds and pounds. I chucked fat coins down the hole and laughed; the hole just got bigger, darker, wetter. I threw drink down my mates' throats and cried, then I staggered home to sleep alone. The thing is if you are born poor you deserve sympathy. But if you had money, if you had money and you threw it away, you are just a sad loser.

When I am at the wall, I never check my balance any more. The last time I saw the dreaded OD numbers, I felt dizzy. I was miserable for a whole Saturday, so miserable that I had to treat myself to a big dirty meringue. That night, I had to drink two bottles of good red wine – can't do the bad – to get over it. Glug, glug. Glug. Now, I can't drink to drown the sorrows because I might drown my baby.

How can a girl who had a piggy bank and a Co-Operative Bank blue savings book and a library card, who helped her mother with the borders in the garden, who planted hyacinths and even once won the school prize for the hyacinth; how can a girl who wore navy gym pants and who played in the school hockey team, who was very good at skipping; how can a girl who blow-dried her mother's hair and shopped with her mother for what they could afford in BHS and Littlewoods, completely lose it, go awol, bankrupt? Do the sums. You do the maths. Do the sums. You do the maths. Dothesumsyoudothemaths. FTSE 100. Datacrash. Fell 82p to 139. Dropped 38.25 to 100.25. Moving down. Lower at 185p. Doldrums for some while. No climbing. Significant negative impact. Stepping down. Who is up? Who is down?

When it comes to it, it is surprising, easy. I leave my house and my belongings – except for a photograph of my mother. (What have my belongings done for me except fill me with a longing for the past? I am tired getting things out of my chest and looking over and over them, as if I might bring the dead back to life.) I have the clothes on my back. I have a small wicker envelope that houses my birth certificate and my passport. I have my mother's smiling face.

I post my key through my letterbox as if I never belonged there, as if I'd just been staying at a mate's house. My baby turns round in my belly and I think it must be her elbow that nudges me, or maybe her tiny foot. There's not enough room for her to move round properly now. In the beginning, she flipped and flashed like a fish. I can't bring my baby into my world of overdue statements. My belly is an enormous skin-tight drum. Boom! Boom. Being pregnant is the one thing I have going for me. Boom and bust.

I am walking slowly down the road from my house into Upper Brooke Street, into Plymouth Grove. I pass a huge pink house. Next to the house, two tall plain trees light up with golden leaves. There are cars in the drive and people going in and out. There's a blue plaque which reads Elizabeth Cleghorn Gaskell 1810–1865. I never knew it was here. I never noticed it before. It seems anybody can go in. Inside there are nice old ladies selling plants. One woman, grey-haired, retired, polite, friendly, says to me, 'When are you due? You look as though it is ready to drop!' I say, 'Any day now.' She smiles at me a little odd smile and then shows me up the rickety wooden stairs into what used to be the caretaker's flat. There's a bright red sixties fireplace. 'If we get the money, we'll rent this place out again,' she says. 'Mrs Gaskell wanted the house to give pleasure. She wanted the house to be used. We only open the shutters on a Sunday. It is such a palaver, opening the shutters. The problem with this house is the drains, there's only two down spouts. When it rains, and it often does, this is Manchester, you get all the water from the entire roof and the drains can't absorb it all.' I nod. I'm sizing the place up the whole time. I've read *North and South*. I've read *Mary Barton*. I've read books in the days when I used to read, when I used to be able to concentrate, before I stopped. When my baby comes, I will read to my baby. I'll start with baby books then toddlers then children's and by the time my child is a teenager, I'll be back to being able to read *Jane Eyre* and *Wuthering Heights* again and maybe something else good that will be written by then.

When I'm leaving I'm already working out my way back in. I take a postcard of Elizabeth Gaskell and stare at her face, walking around the streets of Manchester. It looks kind. I'm tired and my baby is heavy, but I would rather have a heavy baby in my womb than money in the bank, that's for sure.

I wonder what colour my baby will be. At least not the colour of money, thank goodness. I think my baby will have very curly hair, dark hair and very dark eyes. I will simply call her the dark-dark curly-haired one. I don't want her to have a name that they can put a stain against. I don't want her to be in the red.

That night, I return to the Pink House. It is dark. I walk carefully round the back — passing underneath what the woman told me today was the old coach house. I am expecting to have to break open one of the worm-eaten windows, but when I climb the stone steps I notice that the window is propped open with a white chair. I hold the window up with one hand and push the chair out of the way. It's quite an effort. I clamour through with my big tub of tummy. I'm in the room that the woman told me used to be Mrs Gaskell's dining room and study. There's a candle lit and a bed made up on the floor. Next door is the kitchen, there's a tiny table by the window. On it, there's a plate of supper. Some thickly cut bread, some cheese, a small jug of red wine and some water. I wonder who it is who sleeps here, who has made this cosy den for themselves. I sit on the chair near the bed, and listen. Nobody comes. I notice a large feather lying on the bed, big enough to dip into ink, to write a letter with.

Time goes by. The trees outside are still shining in the moonlight, gold leaves. I eat the hunk of bread hungrily and sip the red wine. It won't harm my baby, one small red wine. I stare at the night sky. The little stars twinkle; the clouds are silver-lined. Finally, exhausted, I've never been so tired in my whole life; I lie down in the bed with the clothes on my back. I feel light, actually, light as a feather in the nest. I feel light because the clothes are on my back and my baby in my belly. I feel like I could fly. I could. When my baby arrives, we will live from hand to mouth, from her tiny hand to my full mouth. I don't actually need very much. I need the baby to come and be healthy and I need to put the baby's mouth to my nipple and I need my dark-dark curly-haired one to suck, but nothing else. They won't find me. They will go and take my house. When my baby comes, my life will begin again. I won't get her a piggy bank. Maybe I'll get her a pig instead. A real pig who will look into her dark eyes. Maybe she will love to tickle its big pink hairy belly.

What strange thoughts fly into my head! How will I afford a pig? Pigs might fly. I chortle to myself. For the first time in months I'm not frightened. The future is here and it is not as bad as I thought. If you have nothing, they can take nothing away. I fall asleep, a little wine-happy – it's a while since I drank anything – and before I know it I am dreaming. I am dreaming in the pink house. I think my baby is dreaming too. I know she is.

Grace and Rose

ROSE

Our wedding is drawing nearer and in three peerie days' time I will have married her, after twenty years of saying *I do* and *I love you* in as many ways: in the Shoormal restaurant on the ferry coming back and going away; walking the coast curves along the southern shore of the voe, round the wave-battered Braga Ness; by the great Standing Stone of Bordastubble; in the Wind Dog Café over a bowl of soup in Yell. *Dem at waits, guid befides.*

I wouldn't have believed that we'd ever get a chance to say it in front of other people. I'm already nervous about it; we've been so private for years, so secretive. We started off pretending to be *colleagues* – for goodness' sake! Then we progressed to *chums*. Then it was *best pals* and then we said 'we're like sisters' though of course we were nothing like sisters at all. And then – when would it have been maybe six years ago? – we both told our parents. It was a silly thing because we were women in our late and middle forties, still feart o' telling oor mammies the truth!

When you love somebody, you want your family to love them just as much as you do and of course they hardly ever do, not in the way you want, because nobody measures up. Because the family is its own wee measurement; it doesn't think anybody else fits. But once I saw my mother notice the way that Grace threw back her head when she laughed and my mother smiled alongside her, and I couldn't ask for more than that.

But in three days' time I am to marry Grace, the woman I love. When I first met Grace I felt I had known her for ever and a day. I felt like all my life I'd missed her and now here she was come to be with me at last. I've never felt any differently. Our love is delicate like these islands, a fretwork of rock and heather and water.

At night, I can hardly sleep. We decided we would be apart for this last week. It seems a silly thing to have decided on because we've hardly been separated the whole twenty years. I can't sleep now without Grace. The day of our wedding I'll likely have big bags under my eyes! Oh, well. It's not me that's the beauty. It's Grace. *A bonnie bride is shun buskit*, they say here. But Grace was never interested in marrying a man; once, she said to me she liked the idea of men but not their apparatus! Grace, as well as being beautiful – her grandfather was Italian and she has lovely olive skin and dark black hair and a pretty mouth – has quite a turn of phrase. It's her that has planned our wedding, detail by glorious detail. At first it was great fun planning everything, and then it got stressful and we'd find ourselves waking up in the night worrying about scallops and oysters and flowers and rings. And whether or not we had remembered to invite the local councillor. We'd go for a drink in the Queens and watch the winter sea heave and lash at the old building and count for the umpteenth time our list of one hundred and fifty guests. It was like counting the waves themselves. Old people would be forgotten, new people would be remembered. The list shifted and reshaped itself until we had everybody we wanted.

Goodness me, I said to Grace, knocking back my pint one night, how on earth have the heterosexuals managed all this wedding stuff for years? It could give you a heart attack. It could leave you bankrupt! Grace decided we had a big advantage because both sets of parents would have to pay seeing as we are both daughters, so we can afford to go to town, she said. So – doesn't she want to turn up at Lerwick Town Hall in a vintage Rolls-Royce? (The Rolls-Royce had to be brought from Aberdeen across on the ferry.) Doesn't she want her brother in a kilt and her father in a kilt, and me in a kilt too! She bought me beautiful cufflinks for my shirt, made with opals, my birth stones. And doesn't she want the most beautiful dress, in gold and green silk, handmade for the occasion? Oh, doesn't she want pipers and fiddlers! And why not, my love, I said, perspiring and shaking with fear and anticipation, why not, why shouldn't you have anything you like after all the years we have waited?

'Is it any wonder I've not been sleeping?' I said to Grace. 'Well, if we have all that, we'll have to forgo the honeymoon?' 'Forgo the honeymoon!' she said to me. 'You can't be serious. We'll need a holiday. We'll be exhausted. I'm only getting married so that we can have a honeymoon and so that people can throw confetti as we get driven away.'

'I thought we were getting married so that our relationship can be acknowledged to the world.'

'To the world?' Grace laughed. 'This is Shetland, darling.'

'Yes, well.'

'I'm teasing you,' Grace said, patting my leg and rubbing my inner thigh. She knows if she does that I can't concentrate on anything. Grace knows me through and through. But funnily enough, planning our wedding has shown us both a new side to each other, a more vulnerable, tender side. I don't know how to say it exactly. I tried a few nights ago, I said to Grace, I never knew you were so soft, but that wasn't exactly what I meant. I suppose I never knew that things mattered in the way they matter until we decided to get married. We went out for a walk the last night we had together, a week before our wedding, under the swooning moon, under the sharpest of stars. Do you love me? Grace said. I knew it wasn't a question. It was because she was in love with the words. I do. I do, I said. I stopped and kissed her lips in the cold night air.

GRACE

People are talking. People are talking. Our wedding is the talk of the islands. Those that didn't get invited wanted to be up among da rhubarb. I can't wait to tell you all aboot it. It's a story, our love. We'll tell ourselves the story when we have surprised ourselves by taking up knitting and are sitting watching the tides in Bressay and the fulmar, the puffins, the black guillemots arrive to make their homes in the summer on the east cliffs of Noss. I said, Rose, I never knew you were so romantic. Isn't romance a wonderful thing? Romance is like a wee cove that nobody found but you. Rose makes me feel like the first woman on the moon. We're no that far away from being that, actually: being the first women to marry in Shetland is not so different from being the first women to land on the moon.

I remember the first time I came to Shetland, twenty odd years ago, how strange the peat bogs looked after Glasgow, like something my imagination dreamt up, how astonishing it was never to be further than three miles from the sea.

Let me tell you aboot our day. Both sets of parents were there, all dressed up to the nines. My father in his kilt and long socks and sporran. Oh a man looks handsome in a kilt. Rose wore a kilt too, and I told her to promise me not to wear anything underneath; that was our secret too, the whole wedding day long. Rose looked as if she could die of desire. Was I glad I had insisted on oysters! What an aphrodisiac!

I arrived at Lerwick Town Hall in the Rolls-Royce, a beautiful cream-coloured car. Rose went on ahead with her father so that she would be there before me. My father walked me down the aisle. He had tears in his een. He was proud of me, he said. Prouder than he could be and he never thought he'd see the day, he said, when he would be giving me away. 'I've waited a long time for this, Grace,' he said. Tears sprung to my eyes with gratitude. To think of all the years I worried what he'd think of me!

My father walked me down the aisle and we had lovely fiddle music playing. Aly Bain played a slow fiddle version of 'John Anderson my Jo'. Then we said our vows to each other. Rose said to me: Grace, I love you. I loved you from the minute I met you. I think I even loved you before I met you. I want to walk with you to the end of time.

My mother's eyes filled with tears and Rose's mother's eyes narrowed and sharpened a bit.

I said to Rose: I never thought I would know this in my life, what it is to be loved by you. I want to be loved by you always, for ever, always.

Then Rose put on my ring and I put on hers. Then

we kissed; it seemed the whole island cheered. I imagined we even made the puffins and the whales and the seals happy that day.

Rose and I had the best time planning our wedding feast. We'll all be paying for it until we look like auld fish wives, Rose said, laughing. But it didn't matter. I wanted to have a feast for the whole island to feast their eyes on.

Our feast: five tables, each laid for thirty people, long trestle tables with red crepe covers over each one. To begin with, a soup: smoked haddock, potato and sliced onion soup. Then oysters steamed in almond milk – hand-reared Pacific rock oysters, fresh, plump, very juicy and very clear. Rose and I sucked the flesh out of an oyster in the same pearly minute of time.

Angus, big with a bold stomach, said, 'Do you know there is no way of telling a male oyster from a female by examining their shell?' Nobody really answered him. A few lassies giggled. Then Angus said, 'While oysters have separate sexes, they may change sex one or more times during their life span.' Jessie, Angus's wife, shifted uncomfortably. 'Whit are you saying, Angus?' Angus knocked back his dry Spanish sherry. We were serving small tall glasses of dry sherry with the oysters. Perfect. Then Angus said, 'A pearl is just an irritation for an oyster.' Then the fiddlers started again and the music drowned Angus out. I smiled at Rose and she smiled back at me, raising her eyebrows and shaking her head a little towards Angus.

There was bread flavoured with ale. There were plenty bannocks, gilded peacocks and festooned boar's head, tarts filled with veal and dates, Shetland lamb cooked with fresh coriander, seared salmon with walnuts and thyme, stuffed roast suckling pig, goose cooked in a sauce of grapes and garlic, stewed cabbage flavoured with cinnamon and cloves and grilled asparagus.

For dessert there was fruited custard in huge friendly-faced, born-again pies. We asked our guests to bring small cakes and pile them in the centre of a table. When everyone has finished eating, but not yet finished drinking, Rose stands up and takes my hand and leads me to the table with cakes. She stands around one side of it, fine and sturdy in her kilt, and I stand over the other. We lean towards each other and we kiss, a long, soft, melt of a kiss, and after a minute's lovely silence, everyone cheers. Someone shouts, 'Hurra fir da bride and da bridegroom.' The fiddlers start playing faster and faster and people get up and dance in the middle of the hall. Choocking and whooping and spinning. Hooch! Da whisky wis flowin oot da door.

By the time our wedding feast wis over everybody wis jist pleepin. 'There are days and there are days,' Rose says to me when we drive off for our honeymoon at the Buness House in Unst where we will walk and talk and go over and over our day, telling it in the present tense, in the past. 'Oh, Rose,' I say. 'What if we still hadn't had it yet and we still had our wedding day to look forward to?' Rose groans and shudders, reeling. 'Oh, I'd do it all over again, again and again and again!' she laughs, helplessly. 'I swear the stars look happy for us,' I say to Rose. 'Grace,' she says. 'Oh my dear Grace.'

Bread Bin

It's taken me until the age of forty-nine to have really wonderful sex. I think that's not bad. Some people don't experience good sex until they are sixty. I often see secretly smiling sixty-year-olds when I'm out and about. Then again, some people never have it at all. My grandmother told me she had never had an orgasm. She would discuss sex with a frankness that surprised and embarrassed my mother. Maggie, her good pal, had described an orgasm to her. Maggie says it's kind of a spasm, a great spasm that shakes and shakes the core of you till you are good for nothing. Like a tree in a wild winter storm, a good orgasm could actually uproot you, Maggie had told my grandmother. That was why she left her husband of forty years and ran off with a woman, a womanly woman actually, my grandmother said, with more than a hint of wistfulness. 'The first orgasm of Maggie's entire life uprooted her! She lives down South now!' 'Oh what a shame,' I said, delighted. My grandmother nodded, sipping her tea, a little sorry for herself. Then she snapped out of it. 'It is not one of my biggest regrets – never having an orgasm – if you're good for nothing afterwards,' she said sensibly. Most of her life, she said – her proud neck shaking a little for double emphasis – she was good for something. 'Even my bread bin was clean!' she said, half-angrily, like some women had got away with having dirty bread bins. 'Even the washing on my line was colour coordinated!' Indignant now, like other women had got away with mixing colours up on the line! I tried to look admiring. I was in my early forties when we had that conversation and was beginning to think I'd never find it either. 'What's all the fuss about?' I'd say to pals in similar situations out for consoling meals in romantic restaurants surrounded by sixty-year-olds in love. 'Am I missing something?'

For every lover I've ever had there's been one small defining sexual moment. There was Angie. We were seventeen. I was riding my Honda 50 to her tenement flat in Springburn, Glasgow. (A Honda 50 is maybe not so sexy as a Harley-Davidson, but it felt pretty damn sexy to me at the time.) I was wearing a yellow helmet, dark jeans and a leather jacket. Angie lived on the fourth floor. I ran up the stairs with my helmet still bobbing on my head. Something told me she might fancy me if I arrived wearing it. I was breathing fast through the hole in my helmet. My head felt hot underneath. I didn't know if my feelings for her were right or wrong. All I knew was that they gave me a tight, secret feeling when I was astride my Honda 50.

Angie opened the door and pulled me in. Her eyes were gleaming. I went to take my helmet off and she stopped me. Don't, she said, don't. I like you in that. Look at you, she said. Look at you. She leant in and kissed me through the helmet and then took my hand and led me to her bedroom where she took my helmet off, unstrapping the straps under my chin and lifting my whole hard head off. She laid it down on the bedside table and then kissed me again, slipping her tongue in and out of my mouth, and sliding her tongue over my lips. She undid my blouse and pulled one of my breasts out of my bra and slid her lips over my nipple. I think I love you, she murmured into my breast. Then she sat up. But I love Davy too. Oh, I said, Oh. I sat up too. I wanted to put my helmet on and leave. She pushed me on my back and stared at my belly. Is that a little scar? she said. Yes, I said. And she kissed it.

I left her a few hours later. I was hot and I was bothered. I couldn't see what she saw in Davy McIntosh. He arrived as I was leaving, wearing his Afghan coat with his hair all over his face, smoking his Regal. All right? he said. He was friendly enough. He had a dramatic stammer. Angie said she was going to cure him.

I drove my motorbike home. I had a strange feeling I was being followed. The sky was bright, bright blue. I was in love with a girl who was also in love with a guy, but still I felt like I'd discovered something. Billy Ocean was singing 'Love Really Hurts Without You' inside my head, as I turned left into my street.

My head was throbbing. Love. I kept seeing her face, kissing me. Did she really do that? Did she really kiss my . . . oh my god, she did. She did. I fell in love with the idea of being in love and I think I even liked it when it hurt. The next week Angie said, I think I'll always love you as long as we live, but I only want to kiss Davy now.

I took my bike out for long rides to Fintry and sang along to Janis Ian under my helmet. 'I learned the truth at seventeen that love was meant for beauty queens.'

The next lover was Sally. She was an incredibly quiet person. She hardly spoke. I spent all my time trying to draw her out, open her up. She was so shy; she tied herself up in knots. She'd start a sentence and then get shy of her own sentence and turn back. It was like she was always looking for some brackets to hug her. I feel like, Sally would say. And I'd say – Yes? And she'd say, Never mind never mind never mind. I think I'm feeling, Sally would say another day. Yes?

Well I think . . . Oh, nothing, nothing, nothing. Till one day I said, You are such a tease. And she blushed and said, Oh no, no, no. I'm not a tease. And she pulled me towards her and kissed me, thrusting her tongue right into my mouth. But then when I got into bed with her, I was so surprised. Sally made so much noise having sex, so much noise for such a quiet woman; she almost blasted me out of the bed. I nearly jumped out of my skin when she screamed the first time. I thought something was terribly wrong, that I'd hurt her. After a bit, I realized she was letting all the noise out, all the noise she couldn't make outside of the bedroom. Being quiet as a mouse all day drove dear Sally demented. So it was healthy then, for her to scream her head off in bed. But it didn't do my ears any good and I had to break it to her gently. I was the tongue-tied one now because I knew she had really fallen for me by then. She would have done anything. It's a responsibility being a lover. So it is. I said, I don't think this is working. She said, Tell me what we need to do to make it work. I shook my head sadly and left. I didn't feel all that good about myself. But I didn't feel all that bad either. Life's tough – and I was still young.

Small moments. If Angie was the helmet and Sally was the scream, then Gail was the story. In bed, Gail could only get excited if I told her a story (that she had made up) about a farm hand out in the barn who suddenly came in and discovered us at it in the hay with the nonchalantly placid cows mooing away, close by in the milking barn. Well the farmhand is so surprised and delighted that . . . But I never got further than that bit of the story. Gail would grip me and shudder and shake silently to herself, bending her body over like a half-shut knife, as if in terrible pain.

I began to think that my grandmother was right, that she hadn't missed all that much. The lovers I had either seemed to run away with their orgasms as if they were secret nuts to nibble on someplace far from me, or they shrieked the place down, making elaborate and excruciating expressions on their faces, slapping the bed and slapping me and frightening the hell out of me. Those ones made me feel like I was trapped in some sort of Edinburgh fringe performance show.

Then, just when I had nearly given up, I met her, Martha. We were sitting opposite each other on a train. We chatted for quite a while and I fell asleep for a little dreamlike time. When I woke up, Martha smiled at me. There was something in the way that she smiled — a kind of openness. I knew then. I just knew that I would wake up many more times to Martha smiling at me. We courted for a long time for me — months and months. Drinks, dinners, chats, emails, texts . . . And then one night, she was round at mine, and the thing happened to me. It went all the way through me; it sped back to my birth and hurtled towards my death. It went through me like a train. Like a boat upturning. Like a tree in a wild storm. A couple of days later, I phoned my eighty-five-year-old grandmother to say that her pal Maggie had not been exaggerating. I've got a new woman in my life, Gran, I shouted down the phone. (She was very hard of hearing.) Good, she said — Good. But has she got a clean bread bin?

Doorstep

I've set myself a big challenge this Christmas: I'm spending it alone. There's no point being with people for the sake of being with people. And there's no point buying presents for the sake of it. I'm not good at the presents anyway. I can't get into someone's head to think what they'd like. Christmases past, I've found myself on Christmas Eve spinning up and down Market Street thinking socks, gloves, handkerchiefs, chocolates, bubble bath, thinking what'd she like, what's she not got? It's a bit of a stress and costs way too much. And she always had that look when she opened a present from me, a look on the verge of terrible depression; as if she was thinking you don't really know me, do you?

So: I'm opting out of the whole charade. And when Sharon said, 'Oh let's just get each other something small,' I had to say, 'No, that never works. One person keeps the bargain – under a fiver – and the other one doesn't and then the one that doesn't ends up feeling bitter, and says, "Oh well it's the thought that counts." Like hell! It's the money that counts. It's all gone crazy,' I say.

Sharon pulls a face. 'You're like Scrooge,' she says.

'I'm not. I'm not mean. Look what I forked out on you last year!'

'Oh – are you saying you didn't like *my* present? Is that what this is, Cheryl?' Sharon is indignant.

'No, it's not – but it was a rubbish present,' I say. Sharon looks hurt. 'Joke!' I say.

'How come your jokes are not jokes,' Sharon says. 'How come your jokes are jibes? They're not proper jokes.'

'I'm having a laugh; where's your sense of humour?' I say to Sharon.

'And that's not nice either,' Sharon says, close to tears.

'What's this about?' I say. 'Is this because I'm not getting you a Christmas present?'

Sharon nods, silently, and the tears start to roll down her face. She wipes them away with her fists. 'I didn't mean to cry, sorry,' she says.

'You're a cry-baby,' I say.

'I know,' Sharon gulps. 'I'm a cry-baby.'

'Look, OK then. I'll only get you a present and not my other friends.'

Sharon says nothing, just keeps wiping her tears.

'Is it because you've only really got me who buys you a present at Christmas?' I say. What an idiot I am. Sharon's got nobody. She's big, huge, with massive knockers, and has bad skin and she likes me more than I like her. But I couldn't fancy her in a fit. Sharon doesn't have family; well not any family that she's found anyway. She's been with, I reckon, about twelve foster families. Sometimes I think the only thing that's similar about us is our colour. 'I'm so rubbish,' I say. Sharon starts to smile. 'You're not. It's me. I'm just out of sorts. I've not even got anyone this year to invite me to Christmas dinner.'

'Look, I'll get you a present, but I'm not having you round for dinner,' I say, a bit too quickly.

Sharon really starts to heave, really going for it. 'Don't cry,' I say, half-heartedly.

Sharon talks and cries. It's horrible: worse than somebody talking with their mouth full of food. She half-chokes, half-speaks and the snot is pouring down her face. 'D . . . d . . . d-don't b-b-bother with the present. Don't b-b . . . bother with any of it. You've got no Christmas spirit. And you're not very nice.' Sharon buttons up her navy duffel coat, sniffs and snorts, takes one last sad look at me and leaves my house, quietly closing the door.

Christmas is one way of measuring the year. Last year, at Christmas, I had a partner; I had a job; I had friends. This year, no job, smaller house, and I want to be on my own. She's going to be with her new lover, the Ex is. She'll be doing all that roast bird, potatoes, gravy, pigs in the blanket, honey carrots, stuffing etc. shit for her. She loves crackers; they'll have crackers. She loves roast parsnip; they'll have roast parsnip. Am I bovvered? No, I'm feeling gooooooooooood. I've been liberated from the ordeal of Christmas! Hurray! I can opt out of the fattening Christmas meal, the sodden, shrivelled roasted veg, the Christmas pud – do you have brandy butter or custard, do you microwave or steam – and the wrapping paper, the horrid fights about what to watch on television. I'm having none of it. I'll miss her kids, though. I liked her kids. But at Christmas she spoilt them rotten and there was nothing left for me to get them. That was a stress. That was a big stress: what to get the partner's kids. One year I actually queued from early in the morning for a Buzz Lightyear! It was frantic.

I'll still get the children something and leave it on the doorstep on Christmas Eve; won't matter so much now because the new girlfriend is loaded so I'll go for something very small. Brilliant! I don't think I'm even going to go and get a bird this year. No chicken, no capon, no turkey, no goose, no duck. No three birds stuffed into one. Fabulous! I can say that word like Gavin and Stacey. Fab-lus!

I think I'll get a nut roast. Maybe a nut roast is too lesbian? Something like aubergine parmigiana then instead; something like that. Or I could make a veg lasagne in a small casserole dish, so it doesn't look weird. One thing I've decided is that I'll do the shop soon. I don't want to be in the supermarket with family trolleys heaving with food, and me and my small-and-obviously-alone basket. One of this, one of that – a small carton of milk. I could buy more than I need and freeze the stuff I don't need in case of snow. Or I could

invite Sharon. But I don't want to invite Sharon. I want
to spend the day on my own.

I need to get out of my house and go for a winter
walk. I wrap up well. It's cold enough to snow but the
afternoon sun is shining through the bare trees, like it
has a love interest on the other side of the Ease. How
still the Mersey, today, and dark, like a big mirror. I
stand over it for ages to see if I can see the water move.
People are out with their dogs and their children, their
hats and their scarves and gloves, puffing smoky air out
of their mouths. The clouds are pink in the sky like
candyfloss. It's freezing, but the sun is so bright, it
makes everyone look happy. I can't stop the chatter in
my head. I'd like to be somebody who could simply
walk and take it all in, not be constantly thinking all
the time. I'd like to have a head that is as still as the
winter river. I walk along the river bank, across the
fields and through the woods. At the end of the woods
I spot my first red robin of the winter pecking on the
frozen earth. It doesn't fly off as I get close. It's not shy
at all.

If I don't invite Sharon, she'll spend Christmas on
her own, and I'll spend it on my own. We'll both be in
our different terrace houses. She'll mind and I won't. I
won't mind being on my own. I won't feel the loneliness
that some people feel at Christmastime because actually
I'm quite self-sufficient. That's what my Ex edidn't like

about me. She used to say, 'I wonder if I make any
difference in your life,' and I'd say, 'Not really,' then I'd
say, 'Joke!' But she didn't like my jokes either. I don't
really think my jokes are any worse than the jokes you
find in crackers and nobody seems to mind them; they
just groan – but nobody does that with my jokes.

When I get in from the cold, I take off my scarf that
my middle sister bought me when we were still talking
to each other, and I take off my hat that my Ex bought
me, and I take off my red coat that I bought in Oxfam
in Didsbury. I often wonder about the person who the
coat belonged to; what she's doing this Christmas? I
wouldn't mind that: track down the girl who gave away
the red coat to charity, and offer her Christmas dinner
in exchange for the coat. It makes me feel a bit glam
this red coat. But there'd be no way of finding out. It
does make me realize, though, having that thought, that
I'd quite like a stranger to turn up at the door this
Christmas. Somebody a bit different. A tall dark woman
with a pressie! That would be something! Imagine she
turned up with frankincense or myrrh? Then I'd have to
believe in Christmas. Except: I don't really know what
frankincense or myrrh look like.

It's cold so I decide to put my gas fire on, and I put
the telly on. I have to have something on even if I'm
not listening. There's a Christmas choir singing 'Once
in Royal David's City'. I always liked that when I was
a kid; I used to imagine what the royal city looked like,
crowned in jewels. Sharon thinks it's all about her. It's

not. It's all about me. I decide to ring and tell her.
'I'm sorry about earlier, Sharon,' I say.

'Nothing to be sorry about, Cheryl,' Sharon says.

'I'm just a bit all over the place.'

'We all have off-days,' Sharon says. Her voice sounds
nice and kind. Her voice is nicer than her face. When
you speak to her on the phone, you imagine somebody
quite slim and lovely. 'You have a nice voice, you
know,' I say to Sharon. I manage to stop myself saying
the other part: 'when you hear your voice on the phone,
you imagine someone quite slim and lovely.'

'I was thinking . . . I wonder if you want to come
to mine for Christmas dinner? I mean, I'll be cooking
for me and it's a bit of a waste . . .'

'Oh, that's nice of you, Cheryl, but I've got other
plans now,' Sharon says.

'Other plans?' I say.

'I thought you said you wanted to spend the day on
your own?' Sharon says.

'What's your other plan?' I say. I mean, who does
Sharon have?

'I'm helping in the Soup Kitchen for the Homeless.'

'Oh!' I laugh. 'Well, that's good – easily changed.
Come round for two, then?'

'No, I can't change it,' Sharon says.

'You can't be serious? You'd rather spend Christmas
with the homeless than your mate?'

'I don't want to let them down. Thanks anyway.
What about Boxing Day?'

'All right, then Boxing Day, stay over if you want. Bring your 'jamas.'

Boxing Day is actually just the day after Christmas Day and now that I have company planned for Boxing Day, Christmas Day will pass in a whizz and I can save some of the aubergine parmigiana for Sharon. And actually, it's kind of perfect because it's what I wanted: to spend Christmas Day on my own for the first time in my entire life.

I've bought myself some presents and wrapped them. In the morning, I will get up and put on the television. Then I'll make myself my Christmas breakfast. I'll have the same one that I used to have: scrambled eggs, smoked salmon, Buck's Fizz. Then I'll open my presents. Then I'll watch *It's a Wonderful Life* and cry when James Stewart is happy when the knob comes off the bottom of the stairs. Then I'll try and call my middle sister and wish her Merry Christmas and keep my voice very cheerful. Then I might call my step-father and wish him Merry Christmas. Then I'll slice my aubergine and salt it and leave that for a bit. It's amazing watching the bitter juices come out of the aubergine. I'd like to do that with myself, just pour some salt over.

On Christmas morning, I wake early. I open my pressies and disappoint myself. I should have splashed out a bit more. I can hear that it's snowing outside because the voices are high in the street and I can hear the squeaky, muffled footsteps. I look out the window. I'm right, there's a flurry of snowflakes. Snow is lying thick on the car roofs and on the roofs of the terrace houses. It looks pretty, the thick snow and the red brick, the white snow and the red postbox. I try not to think she is right now having breakfast with the love of her life and I am right now eating breakfast on my own. Sharon could have come, it's my fault. But I had to face it. I had to say to myself, you are alone. You have lost your love. You have nobody to spend Christmas with. And you are having the time of your life. You are. It's wonderful! You can do what you want!

I channel-hop. I laugh hysterically. I sing 'Silent Night' at the top of my voice. I eat a mince pie straight after my breakfast. (I didn't go for the silly smoked salmon in the end – just toast and marmalade.) I sing, 'The holly and the ivy / When they are both full grown / of all the trees that are in the wood / the holly bears the crown.' I dance around my small house. When I catch a vision of me in the mirror with the paper hat from the cracker on – I had to pull it myself; the left hand won, rubbish joke though – I stop and speak to myself, I say, 'This is a blast. Isn't it? This is such a blast.' And then the doorbell rings. And I tear down the stairs. And who should be standing there in her navy duffel coat but Sharon. She's carrying a big bird on a plate and she's smiling sort of a shy smile. There are snowflakes in her hair, snowflakes on her duffel coat, flakes everywhere, melting. She says, 'I did my volunteering on Christmas Eve.' She says, 'Is it OK if I come in, or do you want to be on your own?' I grab hold of her and hug her. (There's a lot to hug.) 'Merry Christmas, dear pal,' I say. 'Merry Christmas!'

Hadassah

Mordecai bring me up like I is his own and in a way I is his own. He call me Hadassah. It mean morning star. He say there is a song about the morning star; he say Hadassah shine a light where no light shine. My parents die when I am little, and that's how Mordecai come. He is not uncle, not cousin to me, more like a father, more like father and mother. Days gone, I smile on my face when we stand by the river. I know my smile is same as Mordecai as he smile back. Look at us in the river, Mordecai say. The river know us. Then I imagine they have another life, the two people in the river; I imagine we leave them there. And when the men take us, and I lose Mordecai, it is there I go in my head — the time by the river. I like to think of a big reef basket carrying Mordecai and me down the dark river beside the river rushes and the lizards, the crocodiles and the logs that look like crocodiles, the white egrets on our tail, white blossom on the trees.

Mordecai tell me I am around fifteen years of age when I am taken away, far away, to another land, a land of milk and honey. When I gets here a man who promise me food and shelter come and meet me. I don't

like the man who name is *the King*. On the day I arrive,
the King is angry with a woman, name of Vashti. The
King is angry with Vashti because she will not do as
he say. He ask her to come to this big do where he say he
fork out good money for the food, and he want to show
her off to the men, name of Pimps. One girl, Nell, tells
me Vashti say, 'I will not eat with men who treat me
like I am a piece of meat.' And that the King get rid of
her; he slice off her head as if she is an egg, Nell say.
He can do what he like, Lily say, the police never come.
Nobody care about us. We are scum. Then Lily starts
dancing round our room singing at the top of her voice,
'We are scum, we are scum, we are scum!' Until Agnes
quiet her and say she is going to get trouble with all
her silliness.

When Vashti leave, or has her head chop off like an
egg, the King send for me! I tremble in his pad – white
and green and blue hangings; tied round his purple
curtain – silver rings. He say let me show you my pad.
His pad is in the same building as the place we sleep,
but it is different from our dump. We never go there
unless he come and take us there or send for us. 'I work
hard for this,' the King say. And he take me to his
kitchen: grey marble top and cupboard and mixer tap.
Then we go into his bedroom and I am embarrass.
On the King's bed is a cover of gold and silver. On his
bedroom floor is a thick red carpet and smaller rugs,
blue and white and black rugs. A wardrobe and drawer
in dark wood. 'See, the furniture is all matching,' he

say. In his living room: leather sofas and big lights and black and white walls with tall marble columns at the side of the room. The King wear a long quilted dressing gown, a dark purple. From time to time, it fall open and I see red Y-fronts.

He say, 'You're going to be *The One* now. Do you know what it means to be *The One*?' I don't know, but I nod because I don't want to be like Vashti and have my head slice like an egg. He say, 'You will be my eyes and ears. Any talk of running off, you come to the King, have you got that into your pretty head, you give the King the nod and the wink?' I nod and he say, speak up. 'You are learning the lingo, aren't you? You know please and thank you?' I say, please and thank you. He laugh; but I don't know what is so funny. He say, 'You never come to me unless you got something to report. Get it? You never come to ask for anything for yourself. Girls that do that get punished. Sort yourself out. I don't want to hear nothing about your problems, got it? You got your periods then get one of the girls to get you tampons or whatever. Understood?' I blush, my cheeks hot. I say please and thank you again. He say, 'I'm trying my best to keep you safe from the Pigs; if you girls don't earn the bacon, how am I supposed to feed you?' I don't understand, so I just say thank you with no please, and he likes that and say, 'You're a fast learner, aren't you, Hadassah?' And he pull my curly black head toward him. And he teach me a new word. After the new word finish, I say, thank you, again and then I leave the Pad quick, back to my dump where we girls, black and brown and white girls, lays in a bed – four or five girls on one mattress on the floor. I lie down on the bed and keep my eyes open, wide as I can.

The floorboards are bare and there is the smell of fear in the room mix with the smell of sweat mix with some horrible smell and nobody trust anybody. I learn the King's English fast so that I can do as the King ask. I learn words I don't want to know the meaning of; I learn words I wish I did not; so many words for the same thing.

Whenever I think the girls are whispering something the King want to know, I lie quiet and listen. I always been a girl who can listen long time and keep still. Quite a few plans, I tell him, and every time I do he give me a gold coin. Know what this is? This is a two-quid coin. I collect my gold coins in a tin. I find a good place to hide them under the wooden floorboards on a low shelf. I am careful nobody is watching when I put a new coin in my tin. I like doing that. I like to count them.

One night, when I am asleep in a huddle with the other girls in our dirty dump, I hear a knocking at the window. I open it and see Mordecai standing on the balcony! Mordecai! He say our people are in trouble; they holding them in Immigration. Mordecai say we must seek asylum. I never know what asylum means then. I still not sure. I know if you go mad you sent to asylum. Mordecai told me the King is a good man, who has his faults and is with the wrong people, but has a heart of gold because he is the one who is help people like us get asylum. At night, I lie awake thinking about this and thinking about the King who help send the women mad. At night in that one room you hear the sound of girls and young women cry, and sometimes pray and sometimes cry and pray together.

I don't think Mordecai really know the kind of man the King is or the kind of things he want girls to do. I tell Mordecai that I learn words I wish I didn't. Mordecai don't understand what I say. He say he has no influence over the King and that I am close, that word on the street say I am as close to the King as anybody. I tell Mordecai, the King say you can't trouble him for nothing or else he will have your head. On day one, he tell me: ask for nothing. Mordecai say, 'Did I bring you up to care about yourself? No, remember our time by the river back in our own country? Remember how you were happy then? One day you will have a decent place again, not like this. You have to be brave and go to the man they call the King and speak up for your people.'

There is eight of us who come from our country. Eight of us who is with Mordecai and me, hidden first as cargo on the boat, and then in a lorry, inside boxes, where we can't breathe, where we think we are going to die, no air, no water, just the dark. We arrive, and a man who is a friend of the King's take me and Mordecai and we never see the rest of our people. 'They were stopped. They didn't make it through,' Mordecai tell me now. 'They have been kept in a holding place.' 'I have not been out,' I whisper to him. 'I have not felt the air on my face. I am prisoner here.'

'You have to talk to the King and get him to help. They need help to fill in the questionnaires.' I shake my head. I can't. I can't. I will get into trouble. Mordecai say, 'Hadassah, remember what I used to tell you when you were a girl, how you shine a light where no one else can shine?' I remember, I say, but in this god-forsaken country, it is each man for hisself. Mordecai look astonish, maybe surprise at my big word. I hear somebody say *godforsaken* the other day and I like the sound of it. I been waiting for a chance to say *godforsaken*. 'Don't you see, Hadassah, if they get them, they will get us. We'll be sent back home where they will find us and kill us.' Mordecai's eyes looked sad and small and black, not like the eyes of the man he is when we stand by the river. Mordecai plead one more time, 'See what you can do.' And Mordecai climb down the drain pipe and vanish into the dark.

The next morning I still don't feel brave and leave my bowl of cereal uneaten on my lap. At lunch time, when our soup come, I leave that too. And at dinner time, when pasta is there, I leave that. One of the girls, Chiamake from Nigeria, notice. She say, Eat your food, girl, or you will starve. Another girl, Betty from Glasgow, say, Are you no wanting this? I'll have it then. And she wolf down my pasta. Next day, I do the same. And Betty wolf my food. Third day – the same, the same. Betty can't believe it! All I have each day is a lemon squeeze into a glass and hot water. Each day I sip my lemon and hot water slow, slow. By then, the hunger gone, and I feel light-head but also concentrate, and I am frighten no more. Not eating make me strong, make me see clearly. Strange it is – nothing in my belly but my thoughts see-through.

And then I ask Clara, who is the one who do the shopping, who is allow out because the King know a girl will not run away because no one has any place to go and even when someone do run away the men find you and sometime Nell say they chop your body into pieces and throw it in the river. They do that even with the small children. Even when they are put in Children Home, they wait and they find them and they steal them away. I tell Clara to use the money in my special tin, my two-quid coins I been saving for *my rainy day*, a rainy day I imagine will change to sunshine when Mordecai come and take me to another place in England; when Mordecai take me where people wear funny hats and push long sticks in the river. I see a picture like that in a mag in the King's Pad.

I give her the coins and I say, Buy food for a party. What do you want? she ask me. So I tell her to get rice so I can make jollof rice, and plantain, and cassava, and chicken legs and cabbage and carrot and onion, pumpkin and black-eyed peas. I say, We can get all those in

England? And she say, *Yeah yeah yeah, course.* You can get anything in England: you can make what you like. You want moyin moyin, cassava, coconut, curry goat, ackee, green plantain, paw paw, prickly pear, egusi soup, collard greens, sweet potato, cocoyam, garri, akara? What you want? Say the word, Clara say, egusi? Just say the word. What in particular you want for the big party? She got so carry away she forgot I tell her already! So I tell her again. I say, Get me some rice so I can make jollof rice and some chicken so I can make fried chicken and some plantain and some collard greens and some cabbage and carrot and onion and salad cream so I can make coleslaw and some black-eyed peas so I can make moyin moyin. Get me some banana leaf. I like to make moyin moyin for Mordecai but he is gone now with disappointment. He does not know my plan. Clara leave the house with my gold coins to get the food for the feast. 'You're crazy?' Lily say. 'Using up all your money like that! It's a waste, girl. What about your rainy day?' But I do not have another rainy day and I have to think how to save my bacon.

The King is out and is coming back with new girls. Out a good few hours. I always feel sorry when the new girls arrive and I see the fear in their eyes and I know the words they are going to learn and what they are going to do with them.

Clara arrive back with all the ingredients she buy from a fab shop in Finsbury Park. Usually Clara come back I like ask her question about Finsbury Park: Can

you see ducks? Are there children on swing? Can you
see big bird? Lots of tree? Did you see yourself in pond?
A picture of Mordecai and me by the river jump into
my mind and I like that. But today, I ask Clara nothing
about the park. I am focus because I fast.

I ask three girls to help prepare the food – Nell and
Lily and Chiamake. I say, Follow me to the King's
kitchen. At first they scare because we never go there.
He never even lock the door he know we too scare. But
I tell them the King say it is ok and they believe me.
'You sure about this?' Chiamake say. 'I'm sure.' Anyway, hunger come first! We pound the onion and the
chilli and add paprika and magi cubes and rub on the
chicken wing and thigh and leg, then fry, then roast;
we fluff the jollof rice, and we fry the plantain and chop
the cabbage and carrot fine-fine for the coleslaw. We
steam the collard greens. I am happy when I see black-
eyed peas. We wrap the moyin moyin in banana leaves
and steam for pudding.

We lay the table with red napkins and silver
cutlery. I am hungry and just the smell of the food feel
like eating. While the chicken roast – before the return
of the King and the Pimps and the new girls – I go
into the King bathroom and pour bath. I pour myrrh
in the bath, lavender oil, sprinkle sea salts – my, how
the King like pamper hisself! – and I wash my hands
and feet and hair and then I dry in the most soft towel
I ever feel. I don't feel worry any more. The fasting
make me brave. I pour bath for Nell and she pour one

for Lily and Lily pour one for Chiamake. It like they are all under my spell. Chiamake say, 'If anything bad happen to us it is worth it to feel clean like this.' Nell say, 'If the King comes back early and is angry that we have taken a bath to clean ourselves for the feast, so be it.' I nod and smile. It is the most happiest feeling I have all the time I am in England. If he is furious and want to hit me; my body can take it. It is strong; it is without food for three days. Inside my head I am the girl of the morning star.

After the bath, I dress in clean clothes that I find in the King's wardrobe, women's clothes that I am surprise to find. And I dress the girls too. We are all ready in our red and purple and black dress, in our silk stocking. We have no shoes, no nice shoes, so we just remain in our stocking soles. We are all waiting. I go into the kitchen and open a bottle of red wine. I find a big jug and pour the wine into the big jug like I see the King do. Then I tell the rest of the women to come and sit round the table and enjoy the feast. They also frighten at first, but the smell of the food change their minds! All the women sit down: Betty sit down first, then Lily, Ruth, Chiamake, Ivy, Clara and Nell and Abigail; Elisabeth and Mary and Hannah and Phoebe and Joanna and Judith; Eunice, Hannah and Anna and the other Anna. All of them gather around the big King table, eyes wide at the feast. All the women, the white, and the brown and the black women, in the big dining room with the oval-shape table and the wall hanging and the rude picture of girls on the wall.

They all look astonish but too hungry to argue. All the women now sitting round the table, all the women from the House of Disrepute. I hear it call that and I repeat it. I say to the women, Let us raise a glass at the table in the House of Disrepute! And everyone laugh and say Thank You. Some say Cheers. Some say Chin Chin. Betty shout Slanjiva! I say, This is a *godforsaken* place, and everyone roar again. Nell say, Hadassah you have some sense of humour. I pour the women some more wine. It is the month of Adar. When the King come back I will make him save our people and I will have revenge for what the Pimps do, the words they make us say every day. I am strong in my head, and I will not forget the words we are force to say and the things we have to do with them. Steady on, Eunice say. We got to remember which side our bread is buttered on, Ruth say. We don't have to remember, I say, and the deep anger in my voice even surprise me. We don't have to remember what the King tell us to remember. We are our own people.

When the King come into his pad, he is going to have surprise, a big surprise. Perhaps even he will astonish. When Mordecai come back and the King been to Immigration to answer the question and our people leave the Holding, I get us out. I make a plan with the women, a plan to get the men who hurt us. They take their life in their hand when they ask for something, you see. I wait to see what the women say. Perhaps it is the wine but suddenly there is roaring round the table, roaring and cheering. Hannah bite her chicken leg; Eunice bite her chicken leg. Everyone laugh. Joanna can't stop laughing till she splutter her wine out on the table. Chiamake say, 'Hadassah, you are a brilliant cook.' 'Thank you,' I say. I wait till everyone has her share, and then I say, 'Lily, please pass me the rice,' and I spoon a single spoon of jollof rice, a chicken thigh, a small spoon of coleslaw. 'Today,' I tell the girls, 'today I break my fast.' 'You have no breakfast so you break your fast,' Nell say because she like words like me, not the kind of word the King teach, but other words, a whole world of other words. Yes, I say, smiling to Nell with some *elegance* (another word I learn and like, *elegance*) my head held high. Today I break my fast. I am Hadassah. My name mean morning star.

The White Cot

It is seldom that Sam and I get away. Sam works long hours and is reluctant to take time off. This time, I think it was obvious I needed a break. I'd been feeling a little down, crying at the slightest thing, and had said often, I think I'm going through the change. I hadn't actually stopped my monthlies, but they were becoming very sporadic.

We arrived at the house around eight in the evening. There was still light in the sky, a brooding light expecting rain. We drove down a long tree-lined driveway to find our cottage at the bottom on the left. Sam unlocked the front door into a large kitchen. At first the house was a disappointment; it struck us as soul-less. 'Don't worry,' Sam said. 'As soon as we've unpacked our things and hung them up, and got our books out, it will feel like ours.' I hoped so. Rented houses often seemed as if they were never truly inhabited. You were too aware of the people who had cleared away all signs of themselves, as if they had never been here at all. There was a feeling of people vanishing that hung in the grotesque decor of the place. Each room was decorated with such purpose that it all felt unreal.

I couldn't imagine the mind of the person who had gone from innocent room to innocent room creating such strangeness.

'Which room shall we pick for our bedroom?' Sam shouted from the top of the stairs. 'Come here and help me choose?' I climbed the stairs slowly, heavily. Why did I think that coming away would make things better? There was a bedroom with pink and yellow wallpaper with a very strong geometric design. 'That wallpaper would drive me mad,' I said to Sam. 'Look, the view from this window is lovely,' Sam said. I looked out; ahead of me was a path, a path that somebody had cut through the long, long grass. The wild grass was full of buttercups and cow parsley and tiny purple flowers: the path cut stretched into the distance and curved towards the east. I could imagine myself walking down it, away into the distance and disappearing off the face of the earth. 'No, not this room,' I said to Sam. 'You choose then, Dionne. I don't mind which room we have. But don't take all day. It's late.'

The walls of the bedroom downstairs were painted a deep red. 'Very sexy!' Sam said, walking into the room. In the corner of the room was an empty cot, an old-fashioned one that had a lace awning over the top like a sun roof. The paint on the bars was scratched a little. The curtains were tied at the sides; it was like a mini-four-poster bed. Inside, there were two soft blankets neatly folded into squares. One was baby blue with a sandy coloured teddy bear stitched in relief. One was pink with a fat white rabbit. There was a tiny white pillow, a white towelling fitted sheet on the mattress and a minute lacy duvet. In the opposite corner of the room was a rocking horse. 'Odd combination,' Sam said. 'We could move the horse out into the kitchen, but we couldn't move the cot.'

'Well, it's this one or the one upstairs,' Sam said and I nodded. I felt like I couldn't speak. Sam went out to the car and brought in our case. 'Why don't you put your feet up and I'll unpack for both of us?' I went into the living room, painted bright yellow and with table lamps covered with feathers. I couldn't shift the uneasy feeling. I sat down on the armchair, cream with red and grey flowers, and then stood up again. I went into the kitchen: yellow painted cupboards, pale blue painted Welsh dresser, black and white floor, navy blue and red small tiles. I stood staring, then put the kettle on. It sounded unnaturally loud. It seemed to go on and on and on, bubbling away furiously before boiling. I could see the water through a window in the kettle splattering against it like rain. I made us both a cup of tea and returned to the living room and sat down. Sam came through and laughed at the expression on my face. 'Don't look so miserable, you're on holiday! Shall we have a leaf through these leaflets and plan our days?' 'Let's leave it until tomorrow,' I said. 'Let's not make plans.'

That night I got into the side of the bed near the window. Sam was already in bed on the other side, book in hand. No matter which house we sleep in, we always choose the same side of the bed; Sam has the left and I have the right. 'You were ages,' Sam said, putting the book down, and curling into me, turning off the bedside lamp. I lay facing out. I lay for the longest time with my eyes open and at some point in the night I felt as if someone had entered the room and gently closed my eyes, tiny fingers, pushing down the lids, pulling the covers over me. I woke up, disorientated with a dull ache in my abdomen. The space next to me was empty. I looked at my phone. It was already ten o'clock. I didn't feel as if I'd been asleep, I felt as if I'd tossed and turned the whole night long, throwing the covers off, putting them back on. At one point in the night, I'd sat bolt upright, drenched in sweat, and full of dread.

Sam had the boiled eggs on; the coffee that we'd brought ourselves, ground with our own grinder, was already bubbling away in our coffeepot. The smell of fresh ground beans was in the air. The half-cut grapefruits were on the table, glasses of orange juice and a jar of our favourite vintage marmalade. There was even warmed milk in the microwave and it was sitting in a jug, painted with cherries and green apples. 'Once you've had your breakfast, you'll feel better. There's nothing like boiling an egg in a place to make it feel your own.' Sam had set the timer on the BlackBerry to get the eggs done to perfection. Sam liked eggs very runny and I liked mine just as they were about to go hard. 'It's one thing we are all allowed to be fussy about, eggs,' Sam was often saying. 'That and how we like our tea; any other fussiness is just neurotic.' The first time this made me laugh, but when it kept being repeated, I wondered what it was really about. Did Sam think I was over-fussy, neurotic?

I sat down at the table and tapped on the shell of my brown egg. I picked the pieces of shell off the top and then broke in. Sam had already been out and got a newspaper. 'Want a bit of the paper?' 'No, thanks,' I said. 'You should take an interest in what's going on in the world, bloody hell; what a mess they've made of Manchester!'

'I've told you,' I said. 'I can't read any more. The words just swim in front of me.'

'You should go and get your eyes checked out, then,' Sam said. 'Often prescriptions change in middle age.' Sam's glasses were tilted on the end of her nose. 'Your glasses aren't right for your eyes,' I said. 'Or you wouldn't be peering over them!'

'At least I can still read,' Sam said and returned to dipping her slice of toast into her queasily runny egg. 'I don't know how you can eat your egg that runny,' I said. 'Leave me and my egg alone,' she said, and shook the newspaper out to find the article she had just been reading. 'Clegg is a pain in the arse; he's duped the lot of us.' Sam sat reading the paper, eating her egg, slurping her coffee. Her thick black hair was a little tousled. She seemed quite content. She looked as if there was nothing the matter at all. I managed to finish my egg and spread some marmalade on a slice of toast and stare into space for quite some time before Sam said, 'Do you want to go for a walk?'

She took my arm firmly and we went out through the pale blue wooden door at the bottom of the garden. We crossed the narrow country road and climbed a wall that had two wooden steps jutting out of it. Then we walked the path that we could see from the bedroom window. At one point we got to a place that we couldn't see from the window, beyond the curve of the path, and I felt like we were suddenly free. 'It's as if that house has eyes,' I said to Sam, 'and now that we are out of its sight-line, I feel suddenly better! Let's stay away. Let's not go back there.' 'You are joking, aren't you?' Sam said. 'You get more and more bonkers every day. I didn't have all this with the menopause you know. I never even noticed it.'

'Well, you were one of the lucky ones,' I said. 'You got away with it. I feel as if I've been stolen and some other woman has been put in my place. I just feel so anxious all the time, like I'm on the edge of something.' 'You'll be fine,' she said as I smiled grimly. 'Well, try and enjoy yourself, why don't you?' Sam said, irritated. 'I mean I've taken all this time off. I've booked us a holiday house . . .'

'It's not work that you're missing,' I said.

'What are you talking about?' Sam said.

'You know what I'm talking about,' I said.

'Oh, here we go! I give up. If you want to see things that are not there, that is your choice,' Sam said. 'I'll

tell you one thing. I'll give you top marks for imagination.'

She walked ahead on the path, big angry strides. I
just stood on the spot staring after her, until she came
back for me. I looped my arm through her arm. 'I'm
sorry,' I said, close to tears. 'You seem so distant, half
the time. I just keep thinking there is someone, even
though of course I know there isn't.'

'You like saying it though, don't you? You like
bringing it up. It's not funny any more, that one.'

'I know,' I said, 'So – what you're saying is there
isn't anyone else?' I was half-joking, but Sam took me
seriously.

'No, there isn't anyone else,' she said, and patted
my arm. She stopped on the path and turned round and
hugged me and kissed my lips, softly. 'I just wish I'd
had a baby,' I blurted out. Sam pulled back. 'What?'
Sam said. 'Where did that come from?'

'I can't stop thinking what my life would have been
like if I'd had my daughter. Do you remember what I
wanted to call her?' Sam shook her head, sadly. 'Don't
go down this path,' she said, 'are you deliberately trying
to ruin our holiday?'

I wanted her to listen, that's all I wanted. 'Here I
am going through this mid-life Hell, and I've got
nothing to show for it. You knew I wanted a baby.'

'Dionne! What's going on? Why are you bringing
all that up? That was years ago,' Sam said. 'Let's go
back to the house! I knew we shouldn't have chosen

that room! Even for me, there's something creepy about
an empty cot!'

'What do you mean, *even for me*, like you're the
reasonable one?'

'I mean, I'm not the one who wanted a baby. Don't
read something into everything! We're on holiday!
We're supposed to be relaxing.' Sam took my arm again
along the last of the path. We came to the bit where
we had to climb over the wall. Sam went first, and
then turned around to help me. I lifted my leg over
and climbed down the wooden step.

'You were the one who chose the house!' I said to
her and the thought startled me. 'You were the one
who looked at the rooms on the Internet. You knew
what was in each room.'

Sam gave me a look that was half fear and half
something I couldn't name. 'I don't know what to do,'
she said. 'I just don't know what to do.'

We walked back to the house. I'd taken my arm
back. The sun was actually out and the sky was really
blue with low-lying white clouds, sweet and innocent
like a child's drawing. 'What kind of mother do you
think you would have been?' Sam said and her voice
was low, and she said the words very slowly with a
space between each word: 'What kind of mother do you
think you would have been?' I said nothing. I walked
behind her dragging my feet and she kept turning to
stare. She looked unhappy; the optimism of the morning had already been knocked out of her. 'Hurry up,'

she said. 'Why do you have to make everything miserable, even a walk in the sunshine?' When we got back to the cottage, Sam unlocked the door, got in a fluster about which key unlocked which bit of the door, finally got us in, and went to the bathroom and slammed the bathroom door shut. I think she cried in there, but when she's like that it's best to leave her alone.

I go and lie down in the bedroom. The more I look at the cot in the room, the more it disturbs me. I start to try and move it across the floor, to see if it will move out of the room altogether and into the other room. But it won't move. It's too solid. 'What are you doing?' Sam says, coming into the room, red-eyed. 'I was just trying to see if this would move!' 'Why?' she says. 'You were the one that picked this room. Do you want to move rooms?' she says. 'We'll change rooms if that will help?' Her voice sounds gentle now; she is trying to make things better. Maybe she regrets her question; I don't know. 'No, that would just be silly,' I say. 'I'll be fine when I feel rested. I'm just not sleeping; it doesn't matter where I sleep with all these hot flushes in the night. I throw the covers off and then throw them back on.' 'Tell me about it,' Sam says laughing. 'I might have to go and sleep in the other room tonight. You were so restless last night; I hardly got any sleep either. I think we're both a bit tetchy today. Shall we start again, darling?' Sam hugs me in a half-hearted sort of a way, as if she must make the best of things.

All day it has felt like I've been waiting for the

night, even though the night and the thought of the
night frighten me, I've waited for it just the same.
When Sam said she would sleep in the other room,
I felt a little hurt, then liberated. It is when I am just
about to have that sensation of somebody coming and
shutting my eyelids with their tiny fingers that I hear
it, the sound of the cot rocking back and forth, back
and forth. It's a creaking sound. I don't dare move
because I want it to go on. I want to hear it. Then,
ever so softly and quite far away, I hear a baby's gurgle
and the sound of chimes, wind chimes. And a strange
little laugh, a merry little baby's laugh, a frothy high
chuckle, delighted and surprised. I get up and walk to
the cot. There's nothing there. There is nothing there,
nothing there at all. I creep back to my bed and listen
carefully as if my life depended on every single sound.
Upstairs, I can hear Sam pad around. It is late for her
to be up. I look at my phone, which suddenly lights
up. It is two in the morning. A bit later, I don't know
the time, I'm sure I hear the front door open.

When I wake in the morning the cot is empty and
the blue and pink blankets are folded neatly in a square.
I'm grateful for the daylight because for a minute I
assume that with it comes normalcy, sanity. I've upset
myself thinking of the baby girl I longed for those years
ago. I even had a name for her, Lottie, and a middle
name, Daphne. Lottie Daphne Drake. I could picture
her. I still can picture her: a head of floppy dark-brown
curls, dark eyes, soft skin, tiny little feet; tiny hands.

A sunny disposition, Lottie had, always gurgling and giggling, curious about everything. And she would have been very quick to learn to say Mama. I thought about her so deeply that I conceived her in my mind. It was a mistake for me to ever name her. I imagined my mornings and nights, my days and evenings, my life; I imagined my life lit up by her life, my daughter's. I imagined how she, little Lottie, would have changed my life. I pictured her so vividly I almost feel that what I went through was like a miscarriage; something I can never get Sam to understand.

'Morning,' I say to Sam, and she looks at me a little warily. 'Sleep well?' 'The minute my head hit the pillow,' Sam says. 'Out like a light.' I wonder if this is really the truth, but I don't ask her. I don't dare say, 'Is that really the truth?'

'I'd quite like to catch up with my old school friend I was telling you about. She's not far from here.' I say.

'I don't think you're up to seeing friends,' Sam says. 'You're acting weird with me, what do you think you'll be like with people you hardly see?' 'I'm making an effort,' I say. 'You told me I should make an effort.' 'Not that kind of effort!' Sam says and laughs to herself, incredulously, a little snort of a laugh.

That day, Sam took me for a drive in the country and I stared out the window. It might yet be all right between us; I might just be going through this change which friends have told me has made them depressed or anxious, paranoid even. 'If only I'd had a baby,' I said to Sam in the car, 'then it would feel worthwhile. I wouldn't mind the hot flushes or the depression if I had a daughter now, a twenty year old daughter or a twenty year old son. Was it that you were jealous of Paul? Is that what it was?' Sam ignored me as if I hadn't spoken and we drove through the beautiful Somerset countryside in silence.

In the cottage that night, Sam made us dinner, spaghetti Bolognese, and opened a bottle of Chianti. She lit a candle. She said, 'Look Dionne, darling, the past is past. We can't do anything about it. I would have loved it if we had had a child together, you know that.'

'A child *together* is what you wanted! You would have liked to have been able to make me pregnant!'

'I would have. Is that a terrible thing?'

'But you couldn't!'

'Thanks for that! Is that my fault?'

'You wouldn't agree to me getting pregnant twenty years ago when there was still time!'

'That is not true and you know it is not true,' Sam said, 'I was happy for you to try with Paul. It was you who didn't want Paul coming between us, not me. Why do you go over the past and distort things?'

'It's not what I remember. *You* didn't want him coming between us!'

'Well, he's come between us and he isn't even here,' Sam said.

*

That night Sam looked over at me sitting in the armchair. 'Dee?' she said. 'Come and have a cuddle.' And I went to her and all the things in my head went quiet for a bit.

'Shall I come in and sleep with you tonight?'

I said yes. I said yes because I wanted her to hear it, to feel it. Sam got into bed with her book and read for a bit and then put the light off. I lay very still waiting for the sounds to start, the wind chimes; the far away baby's gurgle, the sound of the empty cot rocking back and forth, back and forth. I must have fallen asleep. I woke up to the sound of a car in the drive, and then I drifted off again. It was some way into the night before I heard it. I got up and looked in the cot and there was nothing there except the blue blanket had been unwrapped and was not now folded into a square. I shook Sam awake. 'Sam, there is somebody else here,' I said. 'Sam!' She woke up and rubbed her eyes. 'What now?' she said. 'What is it?' She got up and looked in the cot. 'I've seen it all now,' she said. 'You moved that earlier today, didn't you, and now you're pretending somebody else has done it?'

'I didn't touch it,' I said. 'I swear I didn't touch it. I swear on my own life.'

'Well, I bloody well didn't touch it,' Sam said. But there was something in her voice, a belligerence, something a little odd. 'Only you know what you are capable of,' I said and climbed back into bed, and put out my bedside light. I squeezed my eyes shut and lay still waiting to see what she would do next when she thought I had fallen asleep. I had terrible pains in my stomach. After years of being regular as clockwork, it was now difficult to predict.

It must have been sometime later; perhaps two or even three hours later, when I saw Sam tiptoe to the cot. She stood looking over it for quite a while. Then she left the room. Not long after that I heard the sound of the wind chimes and the baby gurgling and I sat bolt upright. I was clammy with fear. Not just a hot flush but the sweat of sheer terror. I got out of bed and crept across the floor as quietly as I could. I peered into the cot. The pink blanket was now unfolded and lying on top of the blue one and the cot was rocking, back and forth, back and forth, with some momentum, and Sam was nowhere in the room. I put my hand to the side of the cot to still it, to stop the rocking and when I looked inside again I saw that the blankets had rolled up into the shape of a small baby and I touched the back and said, there, there. Sam came down the stairs and stood beside me in the semi-dark. She touched my back. She whispered, 'Back to your bed, darling, it's very late.'

The next day, Sam drove me into Bath and we had a bowl of soup in a delicatessen and bought some things for supper, some cheeses, some olives, some salami and bread. 'You look pale,' Sam said over lunch, sipping her strong coffee. 'I so wanted this break to do you good.'

'It is doing me good,' I said and I meant it. I couldn't wait for the night. I'd started not to dread it but to anticipate it, to look forward to it. There was nothing to be frightened of. In the evening we watched a film; a favourite of ours, *An Imitation of Life*. We both wept, as usual, at the end. And again Sam said, 'If you don't mind, my love, I'm going to have to sleep in the other room again. I find all your night-time restlessness a bit exhausting. I'll be back to work soon and I won't feel rested at all. '

'I don't mind,' I said. 'More room for me to stretch out.' That night I didn't lie down. I lay sitting up in bed. I felt a loose feeling and then a letting go. When I got up, the bed sheets were soaked in blood. So much blood, I stared at it appalled as if it was the scene a crime I had committed and couldn't remember. I pulled the sheet off and padded into the bathroom in the dark. I put the sodden sheet in the sink and rinsed it over and over again with cold water. The blood stain wouldn't budge. I found some bleach under the sink and put some of that in. Then I took the whole dripping sheet into the kitchen and put it in the washing machine. I went about the house quietly looking for the airing cupboard trying to remember where I'd seen spare sheets. Finally, I found a fresh one in the bathroom cupboard upstairs. I could hear voices in the other bedroom. I could hear laughing and giggling.

*

I went downstairs to my bedroom again, and switched on the bedside lamp. I couldn't stop crying. I'd lost so much blood, I felt weak. I tried to put the fresh sheet on. It seemed the most difficult task; every time I got it on one corner, it popped off the other. I stared at the cot. The folded blankets were not folded and the little pillow was curled up under them in the shape of a baby. Up the stairs the wind chimes started and the faint sound of the baby's gurgle, then the giggle, then the cot started rocking again, back and forth, and back and forth. I got up and pulled the rocking horse against the door. I pulled two chairs into the room and put them against the door too. I lifted her out of the cot and rocked her in my arms. I started singing softly at first, *Summer time and the living is easy, fish are jumping and the cotton is high. Your daddy's rich and your momma's good-looking, so hush little baby, don't you cry.* There was a pounding on the door. 'Dionne! Open the door! Open the door now!' 'I can't, darling,' I whispered. 'I'm needed here.' Sam pushed against the door and knocked over the horse and the chairs. She stared at me. She said, 'What on earth are you playing at?' 'What are *you* playing at?' I said. 'Well, it's all out now. And I'm getting out. We're going to live on our own, aren't we?' I said to the baby. Sam stared at me and looked as if she was going to faint. 'You're looking very pale,' I said to Sam.

Mind Away

'What was it? If I don't say the minute something comes into my head, puff, it goes,' my mother was saying to me. 'Nope! Gone! The brain's a sieve. Maybe not a sieve, maybe a . . . what's the name of the thing with bigger holes?'

'A colander?' I said.

'Yes, a colander, that's it, the size of the things I'm losing.'

'We're all the same. I'm always forgetting where I've put my keys,' I said.

'I forget more than my keys. It's everything. I'll forget myself soon. I'll forget my head even though it's screwed on. I'll lose myself completely.' My mother started the handbag scramble, frantically searching for something. 'What are you looking for?' I asked her. 'You're always looking for something.' She swung round and stared at me. 'Have you taken it?'

'What?'

'Don't act all innocent with me!' she said, pulling things out of zipped pockets and putting them back in. It was disconcerting. I saw her take her keys out and stuff them behind a cushion on the sofa. Here we go, I said, under my breath. 'I'm forgetting things. I'm losing things. I can almost feel them slipping away, like wee ghosts. Spuooosh, and away they go!'

The interesting thing was that my mother didn't hold on to any emotion for too long, not even anger. She moved quickly, back and forth. I never knew what I was going to get from one minute to the other. 'Do these wee notes to yourself you're always writing not help?' I asked her. 'You know, your *notes to self?*'

'My lists? No! I write things down and then I forget where I've put my list. Did I show you the chocolates Jimmy bought me?'

'You did, yes,' I said, 'kind of Jimmy. Tell me your thoughts and I'll write them down for you. Tell me the minute they come into your head!' I was struck by what a brilliant idea this was. But my mother was not at all keen: 'I know your game. You'll just be writing it all down to make a mockery out of me! Exposing me!'

'I'm just thinking if you could catch them before you lose them you might feel better?'

'It's not so much that my thoughts are running away with me, more like they've run off with somebody else!'

'And who would that be?' I asked her.

'Oooh, a young, dishy doctor,' my mother said, without a moment's hesitation.

'We'll need to do a bit of private investigating and see if we can track him down,' I said. 'We'll go out later today and we'll track this doctor down.' My mother giggled, clearly delighted. I put a clean piece of A4 paper in my old Olivetti and typed Doctor runs off with an old woman's thoughts. I poured myself a small malt: a childhood smell from the pine woods, a wood smoke fire outside, a black stick of liquorice. I think I could smell the smell I used to smell on holidays in Yell, a smell of peat bog. I remember my mother and me in the Windy Dog Café eating soup, not that long before she lost her marbles.

'Here you!' my mother said. 'Is it not a bit early for the whisky? It's light out there.' Strange how some things still didn't get past her. 'I'm forty-four!' I said. 'It's cold outside, nothing like a wee nip to warm you up. Besides, all private investigators keep a bottle of Scotch in their seedy offices!' My mother's eyes shone. 'This is the best idea you've had in a long time!' she beamed. 'What would we call ourselves?' 'Nora and Mary?' I said. 'What are you saying?' my mother said irritably. 'What we'd call ourselves,' I said. 'Or maybe surnames are better for detectives, maybe Gourdie and Gourdie, how about that?' My mother looked at me blankly. I'd lost her. No one in! But two minutes later she was back again, surprising me. 'I'm certain he'll be an NHS man. He'll not be a BUPA doctor! Not in a million years! Come on, Nora Gourdie,' she said to herself, trying to put her tights on, rolling them over her fist and aiming her flesh foot into the foot of her opaque tights with reinforced toes. I kept typing away; it was the only thing that stopped my migraine, paradoxically, the sound of typing. Sometimes, I'd find myself typing a sentence that would surprise me: 'I've lost the will to live,' he said.

Doctor Mahmud was sitting in his surgery with a patient, Peter Henderson, when Doctor Mahmud suddenly said, 'I'm finding I don't like wearing tights any more. It's a hassle pulling them up and over my ankles, my knees. I'm that exhausted when I've hoisted them over my knickers that I've lost the will to live. Time *Sheer* and I parted company!'

'Excuse me, Doctor?' Peter said. Doctor Mahmud had just finished writing a prescription in his rather erratic and mostly illegible handwriting. Peter Henderson was fifty-six, and had been told his cholesterol was sky high and he would need to start taking cholesterol pills and cut down on certain foods. Peter was feeling morose, and a little jumpy. 'Sorry?' Peter said. 'What were you saying?' But the doctor stared at him blankly as if he hadn't said a thing. Just being in the doctor's surgery reminded Peter that he was going to die. All right, not for a while yet, but it was going to happen. It wasn't kidding on, death. It would come for him, like it had come for his mother, his wife, his old pal Duncan.

Doctor Mahmud was a handsome big bugger, slim, fit, sympathetic, usually. Peter Henderson was hefty; he barely fitted into the patient's seat. He perched on the end of it and waited for the doctor to speak. He sat with his legs splayed open because they were too fat to close. He'd been brought up to revere a doctor. The thing about this cholesterol was that you couldn't eat any of your favourite things any more, which made you wonder not if life was worth living exactly, but if life was rich enough to live, if it had enough flavour. What was the point in going through the motions of life without deep-fried Mars Bars, bloody steaks, streaky bacon and eggs, a poke of chips and curry sauce? The future was oily fish, spinach, rocket, watercress, Christ! 'It's all about unsaturated fat,' Doctor Mahmud said. 'I'll Google fat when I get home the night,' Peter said, in a thin voice. 'No. Google makes people paranoid. Too much information! Stay away from Google!' 'Right,' Peter laughed a little nervously. What was it with the doctor today? Was he just going off on one? 'There's really nothing to worry about,' the doctor said, frowning. 'We'll do another blood test in six weeks to measure your levels again.'

'Thank you, Doctor. Will the pills have any side effects?' Peter asked, staring at the weighing scales in the surgery, and feeling a moment's relief that he hadn't been asked to stand on them. 'No, you won't notice anything. There are people with worse problems. Cholesterol? Many people have high cholesterol. Eh? We're living in the age of cholesterol. This is not the age of Aquarius!' Peter laughed, not his usual big booming laugh, but a little squeaky, *eee hee hee*. His beer belly hung over his trousers. Little beads of sweat assembled on his forehead. He was just about to lumber himself out of the seat when the good doctor suddenly shouted: 'The snags, the rips, the ladders! Why did any of us bother? Why didn't we wear trousers years ago? Knee-highs, that's what I need, a thin pair of knee-high socks! That would sort me out.' 'Excuse me?' Peter said again to the doctor, thinking perhaps there was also something going wrong with his hearing. These days when Peter watched the television, particularly soaps, he heard a small voice underneath the actors whispering stage instructions. *Maria closes the door and walks to Underworld, the knicker factory.* The doctor's white coat, his stethoscope, his blood-pressure pump, his neat desk, all of that was the same as usual, but what was happening to the doctor's conversation?

Peter looked at the people in the waiting room. Little do you know what you're in for, he thought, looking at the anxious young mum with her snotty-nosed baby. He popped his head through the reception hatch. 'Doctor Mahmud says another appointment in six weeks?' the receptionist said. Peter nodded and sighed, a single tear trickled down his ruddy cheek. He picked up his prescription and exited the surgery so fast he was sure that he could feel his cholesterol level hitting the sky.

Alone in his surgery, Doctor Mahmud washed his hands with surgical cleaner at the small, low sink in the corner of the room. He dried them on a paper towel and looked in the mirror. His hair was neat enough; his small beard was well trimmed; his eyes were a little dark underneath. He was trying to think when it first started. There was nothing in any of his symptoms that he recognized. He was thirty-three years old, and was enjoying being part of Springfield Practice. He worked alongside two brilliant doctors. (Though Mahmud would have to admit – if pushed – that he was the most popular of the three; patients clamoured to see him.) If it happened again, he'd have to go and see somebody.

'Mary, do you think,' my mother was saying to me, 'that if I found the right doctor, I'd get my train of thoughts back?'

'I hope so, Mother!' I said.

'You gotta hope!' my mother said, bursting into song. 'You've gotta live a little, love a little, make your poor heart . . . a little, that's the story of, that's the glory of love. You gotta hope!'

'Hope's our only hope, Mother,' I said and knocked back a little more whisky.

'Whisky is not hope!' my mother said, her beady, demented eyes still taking in my wee dram.

'Maybe not, but it's full of character,' I said.

'Pass me the Yellow Pages!' my mother said, impatient and somehow suddenly authoritative.

'Where there's life, there's hope,' I said.

'There's life in the old dog yet,' my mother said.

'Who was your favourite dog of ours?' I asked her. She seemed to have no trouble remembering the past.

'Dinky!' she said instantly. 'Do you remember dear Dinky, those serious eyes, that sad-looking face? Remember how she'd eat the post? Love letters were always arriving with bite marks in them.'

'What love letters?' I said. My mother started up the handbag scramble again, frantic, distressed. She found a lipstick in the bag, and slashed it inaccurately across her lips. I got up from the typewriter, took the lipstick out her hand, wiped it off and reapplied it. 'Then there was Gatsby! Remember Gatsby?' my mother said. 'Remember the Gatsby era? That time he fell off the wall into all that mud. I could measure my whole life in dogs!'

'Gatsby wasn't that long ago,' I said. 'Gatsby just died last year.'

'Did he?' my mother said. 'Very sad.'

'It's a dog's life!' I said. 'Remember how you could never throw away the leads of our dead dogs? They'd still hang up on the hook on the kitchen door?' I said. 'No point chucking out a good lead.' My mother chuckled. Word association, I thought to myself. She can do word association. The migraine was on its way out, hopefully, though I still felt a little queasy; perhaps the whisky would settle my stomach.

'Who thought up the name Gatsby? Remember Gatsby. Gatsby was a Dalmatian. I used to have a beautiful black and white polka-dot dress exactly like that dog's spots. Your mother was a snazzy dresser!'

'I remember. You still are. You're trendy. You wouldn't be seen dead in a twinset!'

I flicked through a lifestyle column in last Sunday's paper. 'What happened to that dress?' I asked. 'One night your father took me to the Locarno. I remember I was wearing it then. I felt good in it. I felt like a million dollars. We danced and danced and danced. Your father could move,' my mother's eyes filled with involuntary tears. That happened these days, these nowhere tears. 'Aye, Billy was a wonderful dancer,' my mother said. 'Billy?' I said. 'Who is Billy?' 'Did I show you the chocolates Jimmy brought me?' she said, gathering herself. 'You did yes, very kind of Jimmy,' I said. 'Did you thank Jimmy for the chocolates?' My mother looked wild, worried. 'I can't remember,' she said. 'Oh, I must thank Jimmy. Oh dear, I must thank Jimmy.'

I went back to trying to read an article in the mag. It was an article on how well Meryl Streep has aged and how many different parts she's played. 'You'd never think Meryl Streep was just ten years younger than you,' I muttered, though my mother's face wasn't very lined. 'Botox! Is she on the Botox? Or is it the liposuction? What's the difference again? Does one put things in and the other suck things out? That's what's happening to me. My mind's lip sucked! Yep. My mind's lip sucked!' my mother said. In her own way, she was wildly funny. I sipped at my dram. 'Maple syrup, maybe, anyone?'

'What are you saying?' my mother said. 'It's just gibberish. I've enough gibberish in my head without you talking gobbled gook.'

'Gobbledy gook!' I said. 'Anyway, I think we need to get out and into the day before you start telling me it's my fault your brain's scrambled.'

'We need to find him first or we won't know where to go!' my mother said.

'Who?' I said, blankly.

'The doctor! That's who. Doctor Who!' my mother said, impatiently.

'Just testing,' I said.

'You were not. Your brain's addled. That whisky is not your friend. It is your enemy. Where's Becky? She was always telling you to have dry days.'

'Becky and I are finished, Mum. I keep telling you. It's over.'

'Oh dear,' my mother said for the umpteenth time. 'I was awful fond of Becky.'

'She's bought me out,' I told her again. 'That's why I'm here. I'm waiting for my new house to come through.'

'Are you?' my mother said. 'Are you staying with me? Is there no chance of reconciliation?'

'No! No! NO!' I snapped. 'How many times? We're finished. We're so over. I don't think we'll even manage to be friends.'

My mother had a look on her face that seemed already to be forgetting what I'd just told her, though her face still appeared distressed, but now the distress was unspecific, vague, a spread of general anxiety. She flicked through the Yellow Pages at a ferocious speed.

I went back to my typewriter. Doctor Mahmud picked up the telephone on his desk. He'd already forgotten what he wanted to say. He looked at his notepad, confused. 'Hello? Is that the Memory Clinic? My name is Doctor Mahmud from Springfield Practice. One of my patients seems to be losing his memory. What's the procedure for making an appointment?' My mother was still trying to make sense of the Yellow Pages, a hard ask for any of us, never mind those with dementia. 'The letters seem all jumbled! Why do we have to suffer from old age when we are elderly?' my mother said. 'Because you're old, Mother,' I said. 'Yes, but it'd be better to suffer from old age when you were young enough to cope with it.'

'Oh, you come out with some loo-loos,' I said. 'Some real beauties.' 'It takes ages to remember what letters come where these days! When you were younger, the alphabet was a skoosh; mental arithmetic was a doddle. I blame the government,' my mother exclaimed. 'You've lost me,' I said. I was trying to guess her meaning – The banks bail out? The recession? Student fees? Teaching standards? 'They've made infants of the lot of us! Soon we won't be able to eat without the food beeping. No one can do a bloody thing! You can't get into your car without the bloody beeps coming on if you've not fastened your seatbelt. What if you don't want to fasten your silly seatbelt?' she shouted. 'What if you'd prefer to take your chances? I'll tell you . . . I'm telling you! . . . Did I show you the chocolates Jimmy bought me?'

'Very kind of Jimmy,' I said. 'I'm quite peckish,' I said, hinting heavily.

'Can I test him myself?' Doctor Mahmud was saying on the phone. 'How can I tell if it's Alzheimer's or dementia or depression or a brain tumour?' He listened for a minute. 'I'll try that and get back to you. Thank you. No chocolates the day! I'm not hungry,' he suddenly blurted out. 'Sorry, I was just talking to my receptionist there. Thank you for your help,' Doctor Mahmud said and hung up abruptly.

'Time for Mozart!' I said to my mother. I'd read somewhere that listening to Mozart slowed down Alzheimer's. At least I think I'd read that; I couldn't be sure. I was forgetting things myself. I put on Mozart's trio for clarinet, viola and piano in E Flat, K. 498. It consoled me that Mozart was said to have composed this during a game of skittles. My mother sat and listened with her eyes closed, the Yellow Pages on her lap. A little tear rolled down her face. Music moved her. I imagined my mother dancing, years ago, dancing in an elegant polka-dot dress. 'Mum,' I said, gently, 'was my dad your only love?' She didn't open her eyes. I pressed pause when the piece was finished. Our lives

had turned around: I used to love *Watch with Mother*;
now I loved *Listen with Mother*.

Music seemed to work every time. She always remembered what she'd just been doing. 'Bishopbriggs?'
my mother said, pointing her finger at *Springfield Health
Clinic*. 'Why don't we try the good doctors of Bishopbriggs?' she said. 'I like that,' I said and made a note
of it in my notebook. Even demented, my mother's
impromptu titles were better than my own. 'Years ago
I remember going for dinner in a place called Stakis
in Bishopbriggs with my pal Nancy Henshaw. I had a
gammon steak with pineapple and Nancy had scampi
and chips. We were over the moon. We thought we
were the peak of sophistication!' My mother was laughing at the memory of herself when her hair was darker
and her teeth her own and her mind, her mind agile,
quick as a young hare running over a field of bluebells.

'You remember years ago with uncanny detail,' I
complimented her. '*Years ago* is not the problem. Yesterday is the problem. Today is the problem. Years ago
are piling up! Who do you think put gammon steak
and pineapple together? I'll tell you one thing, it
wouldn't have been the Prime Minister,' my mother
said. 'It wouldn't have been Cameron.' 'Maybe it was
the opposition,' I said entering into the spirit of things.
'Maybe it was Clegg.' 'I get you!' my mother said,
nudging me fiercely with her right elbow. 'Eh?' she
said elbowing again. 'Opposites attract!' I said, smiling.

'Well, your father and I were definitely opposites,' she laughed. 'I was good looking and he wasn't.' The tears poured again. 'Have you found him yet? This handsome doctor?'

'The last Sunday of every month, I gave his eye-brows a good plucking, you know, to keep him ship-shape,' Doctor Mahmud blurted out in his surgery. He frowned and paced the room, shaking his head. He flicked through his medical books talking to himself all the time. 'Blurting out random sentences?' He sighed and rubbed his hands together. 'Right! You can combat this. You're young. You're smart. You're a doctor.' He sat back down at his desk and ran his fingers through his hair. He picked up a pencil and showed it to himself. 'What is this called?' he shouted. 'A pencil!' he answered. He took off his watch. 'And this?' 'A watch.' 'Repeat after me: no ifs and buts.' 'No ifs and buts,' he repeated. 'Repeat after me: ball, car, man. Spell WORLD.' 'W-O-R-L-D.' 'Spell World backwords!' He stumbled a bit, and shouted out in frustration, 'Bloody hell. D-L-R-O-W!' 'What three words did I ask you to repeat? Car, ball, man. Car, ball, man.' The doctor's relief brought him close to tears. He grabbed a sheet of paper from his desk, folded it in half. Knelt down on the floor and asked himself, 'Can you draw the face of a clock?'

'I was asking you something,' my mother said.

'You were asking me if I'd found the handsome doctor yet.'

'That's it! Well, have you?'

'Well . . . we can't tell if they are handsome from their names, unfortunately,' I said. I smiled, a silly little smile; I could feel it on my face. I could feel the good heat from the whisky in my stomach. My stomach was nice and empty so that I'd get the full hit of it. There was a kind of a roar as it went down, like my body was a furnace and I was throwing the flame in. 'Well, let's take pot luck then. Someone's got to know something,' my mother said darkly. 'You can't just have words disappearing in the dead of night and nobody bothering their shirt! Someone's bound to have noticed something! Somewhere!'

'Ha!' I said. 'Absolutely!' I was thinking what lovely company this Alzheimer's was for my drunken paranoia.

My mother was reading names out: Dr B. Gordon, Dr C. Berg, Dr I. T. McNicholl, Dr Robert Mair, Dr P. MacBrayne, Dr M. Mahmud. 'How about we try all of them?' I said. 'How will I know which one to pick?' my mother said anxiously. 'It's not you doing the picking! He's already chosen *you*, this doctor who-ever he is! He's already *got* your thoughts!' I said, feeling inspired. 'Oh, you're right,' my mother said, gripping my arm. 'You're not wrong. What a moment of lucid-ity! Right, let's get out there and find him. What have we got to lose? Isn't life an awfully big adventure? Who was it who said that again? I've forgotten.'

These days we were spending so much time stand-ing in the street — my mother trying to remember where it was she wanted to go. The day before, she had been determined we went to her church for a bowl of soup in the church cafe. I had never been to her church and had no idea where it was. I was a non-believer anyway. She'd changed her faith when I was a teenager. We stopped and asked a policeman for directions; he leaned out of the window of his police car and looked into my mother's eyes. If only we could go to Lost Property and claim her mind back I thought; if only it'd been left at Left Luggage. The policeman didn't know; there were three churches nearby, and my mother couldn't remember the name. So we went into her hairdresser's at the corner of our street, and asked them. 'Excuse me?' my mother said. 'Where is my church?' The hairdresser shook her glossy hair and looked a little nonplussed. We left. 'It's like our own little pil-grimage,' I said to my mother, consolingly. She was very agitated. 'Oh, your father would be angry with me by now.'

'Don't be silly, it's an adventure, our awfully big adventure,' I said. 'Who said that again? Did somebody just say that?' she said. I put my arm through hers and we walked along the street adjacent to her house. The trees were losing their leaves, the birds were losing their feathers, the pound was losing its value and my mother was losing her mind. It was cold, freezing cold. 'We're in for a cold snap,' my mother said. 'I think it might snow later.'

Eventually we found it, and we had our bowl of

soup and she beamed with pleasure. 'Nora enjoys a good bowl of soup,' my mother said. She loved characterizing herself in this way, as if she was somebody else – perhaps she was now. The soup was religiously good – barley, carrots, potatoes, and chicken. 'What's the name of these wee soft bits?' she asked me.

'What was I going to tell you?' my mother now said and shook her head, looking a little stunned, surprised at herself, as if on the edge of something uproarious.

'Do you remember we went out yesterday to find your church?' I asked her. 'No,' she said. 'Well, did we find it?' 'Yes, we did and we had a bowl of soup.' 'Did we?' my mother said. 'Did we have soup?'

Doctor Mahmud said to the young mother with the baby on her lap, 'There's nothing like a good bowl of soup. It warms up the old heart. Mind, you've got to cut the pieces wee enough. You dinny want to choke on your soup!' Then he got up abruptly, troubled, and washed his hands. He washed his hands over and over again. The backs of his hands were very hairy. More hairy than usual? He wasn't sure. It was no joke now. 'I think she's too young for solids,' the young mother said. Her baby was ten days old. Doctor Mahmud ran his fingers through his hair. He would have to take some time off. He couldn't go on like this. So far there'd been no complaints; but it was only a matter of time. The doctor would have to get to the root of it. You couldn't practise as a reputable GP shouting at people in this manner! It was appalling. It was against everything he'd been taught. He turned back around and put his thermometer under the baby's arm. The baby was crying, a high-pitched newborn's cry. It set his teeth on edge. 'Barley! That's the name! Barley!' he shouted over the din of the greeting bairn. The baby stopped crying instantly. Out of the blue, there was a lovely spacey silence in the surgery between the baby, the doctor and the mother. The doctor looked out of his window. Snowflakes drifted dreamily and the doctor said pleasantly, 'Plenty fluids, no cause for alarm. You're breastfeeding?' The mother nodded, wide-eyed. Everything about being a new mum was terrifying. The world was suddenly a terrifying place. Even the doctors were scary. She found herself bursting into tears when she watched the news. What had she done bringing a baby into a world like this? 'Doctor,' she said, tentatively, 'I'm feeling worried about the world.'

'This is normal. All new mums want world peace!' Doctor Mahmud said, laughing bravely.

'I'm worried she'll grow up in a world where she'll never see a panda,' she cried. The tears rolled down her cheeks. 'Don't worry.' For the first time that day, the doctor could feel the other voice coming on. He had to get her out of the room before it spoke again. Maybe this was a good sign. Maybe it meant he could exercise some control. He ushered the young mum to the door.

It was strange. It felt as if it was getting closer, and the instances were becoming more acute. He had a sense of what it must be like being in labour – the panic of the contractions coming quicker and quicker. The mum was still talking. 'I'm finding I can't sleep at night for worrying about what's going on in the world. Bad news, bad news. It gets right inside my heid.'

'Turn the TV off!' the doctor snapped. 'Jumpy mummy, jumpy baby eh? Your baby is fine. Keep an eye on the fluid intake.' He held open the door pointedly. 'But she's growing up in such a cruel world. I'm feeling like we're all doomed. There's nothing to hope for. Pity you can't write me a prescription for what's going on in the world, for all the fear and worry.'

The doctor put his foot in the door to keep it open. 'Wish I could. If I gave you a sedative, it would sedate your baby. Druggy mummy, druggy baby, eh?' The young woman left and Doctor Mahmud sighed with relief. He walked back to his desk, shook his head. 'What day of the week is it?' he asked himself. 'Wednesday.' 'What is the month?' 'January.' 'What is the date?' 'January the . . .' 'What town are we in?' 'Glasgow.' 'What county?' 'Scotland.' 'No! What county?' 'East Dunbartonshire. We're in East Dunbartonshire.'

I took the sheet out of the Olivetti. It hadn't quite worked the way I'd planned. The only thing that was consistent was the way the letter h was missing in the

Olivetti, it tried to hit h, but then only left a ghost of an h there. The trut was I was terrified, terrified of losing my mot er, not of er dying but of losing er because s e was losing erself is ow t at sentence would look if I typed it out. It was ard to keep track of w at I was saying wit t e missing.

Before we left for Bishopbriggs, my mother had a panic over her keys. I fastened my seatbelt and got ready for it. 'What have you done with them?' she asked me. 'With what?' I said, though I knew of course what she was talking about. 'My keys, Diddy!' she said impatiently. 'I haven't touched your keys. You're always accusing me of hiding your keys.'

'No one else is in the house. It's got to be you. Why do you do it, Mary, why oh why oh why.' My mother started to cry. 'Don't upset yourself, Mum,' I said. 'Anyway, I've got a spare set.'

'I want my own keys,' my mother wailed like a baby.

'Well, let's see where you've put them this time.' I hunted around for her keys. I'd seen her put them behind the cushion on the sofa earlier but I didn't want to find them too quickly. My mother started the handbag scramble and I tried to take the bag and look for her. She tussled me for it and everything fell onto the floor, all the rubbish she keeps in there, the hairpins and receipts and old photographs and letters.

'Now look what you've done!' she said.

'I am not going to steal from you, Mum, I'm your

daughter.' I was close to tears myself, filled with fury and frustration. It was all so hopeless. My mother seemed to notice and softened. 'My keys have mibbe been burgled so that they can burgle me later,' she announced.

'Who?'

'Them,' she said darkly.

'Things have been moving about. They've been listening to me on the phone. They know when I'm out.'

'I think we should go out now, before it is too late,' I said. The afternoon will go and the dark will come down and then we won't get out, and then it will be another day, I thought. I knew I was in for a period of darkness. My mother pulled the cushion back on the couch and discovered her keys. 'Found them,' she announced. 'Why did you put them there? I would never have put them there,' she said.

'Never mind, you've found them now,' I said. 'Let's go.'

'My keys need to go in my zipped pouch,' my mother said.

'Put them in your zipped pouch, then,' I said, tired.

My mother and I got off the train at Bishopbriggs. From Glasgow Queen Street to Bishopbriggs Cross was just seven minutes. We crossed over the railway bridge and walked down the slope at the other side. 'Where's Stakis? Can we find Stakis and have a gammon steak and pineapple?' my mother said. 'After the doctor's!' I said firmly. (I didn't want to tell her that Stakis wouldn't be there any more.) 'Oh yes, the doctor's. I forgot. I can picture him,' my mother said. 'He's handsome. He's Pakistani. He's got a small beard. He's tall. He's kind. He's got beautiful eyes. And a lovely set of teeth! His smile would melt an old woman's heart.' 'Goodness! I hope he exists!' I said wryly. I was starting to feel panicky. How would I get any new doctor to see my mother? How would I explain her thinking about her lost thoughts? It was crazy. I should never have indulged her. I'd gone too far. 'He exists, all right,' my mother said walking quickly up the road. There was nothing wrong with her mobility. She was faster than me. I was finding walking in a straight line a bit of a challenge. If my mother got her lost thoughts back, I'd give up whisky! That felt like a decent bargain. Three cars were waiting at the traffic lights under the old railway bridge. The lights changed.

'When we get there, you let me do the talking,' I said to my mother. She nodded. 'I'm having the time of my life,' she said. 'We're cannier than Cagney and Lacey; we've got more irony than Ironside, we've got more hair than Kojak, nicer raincoats than Columbo, better sweaters than Starsky and Hutch,' I said, laughing. 'But we're not more stylish than, what's her name? Oh damn, it's gone. What's her name; you know the one, the one that had the wee drunken dance with her whisky?' my mother said.

'Helen Mirren! *Prime Suspect*! Prime!' Doctor Mahmud said aloud to the mirror in his surgery. 'One of they women that looks as if life's begun at sixty, like sixty is the new forty. Sexy, sexy! Some figure on her.' He called reception, really disturbed now. He looked at the hair on the backs of his hands as if he was physically turning into somebody else. He suddenly decided to shave his beard off. Then stopped, his face full of lather. He pressed his buzzer to the reception: 'No more patients for me today, please. I'm not feeling myself. Can you get Doctor Gordon and Doctor Berg to relieve me?' The receptionist sounded frazzled. Doctor Mahmud flicked the switch. The receptionist pulled a face. Weirder and weirder! Outside the surgery, snow had started to fall in earnest. Doctor Mahmud's hand was steady as he took the razor blade across his chin. 'It's snowing,' he said out loud. 'It's actually snowing.'

Nora Gourdie stuck her tongue out; she pulled the red scarf around her neck tighter. 'It's snowing,' she said. 'It's actually snowing.' Snowflakes melted on her tongue. 'Do you think it's going to lie?' she asked her daughter. 'I hope it does. It's lovely when the snow covers everything, pretty, eh?'

'We are here,' I said. The snow was whirling now, dancing. I was feeling like a complete idiot, bringing my old mother out in the freezing cold in a flurry of flakes in search of a Pakistani doctor. It was insane. It was another sign for me, that I was knocking it back too much. I'd lost all sense of judgement and propriety. 'You sit there,' I told her. 'I'll go and see what's what. You're going to come as a bit of a shock to him if he is here.' My mother nodded. Her eyes were shining. 'What if I fall in love with him?' she said. 'Oh, the snow's so romantic! The age difference will just melt away. Love does not care about age difference!'

'Excuse me,' I asked at the reception, speaking softly. 'I wonder if you can help me? My mother's got what we think might be early onset Alzheimer's or dementia. We're not sure. And I wondered if she could see a doctor here? We're visiting Bishopbriggs, you see, staying with friends. We've come down from Ullapool,' I lied.

'I'm sorry,' the receptionist said. 'We're inundated the day.'

'That's him! Look, there he is!' my mother shouted, springing to her feet and pointing excitedly at a tall handsome man leaving a room with a pile of files in his arms. 'Is he a doctor?' I asked the receptionist. 'Yes, that's Doctor Mahmud, but he's not feeling well. He's going home early.'

'Do you know me? Do you know me like I know you?' my mother was saying. Doctor Mahmud stared at the small woman with grey hair, her red coat. There was something familiar about her. She wasn't one of his patients, he was certain of that. It wasn't her face that was familiar. What was it? He stood staring at her, puzzled. 'He's the one! He's the one!' my mother shouted. 'I'm so sorry about this,' I said, approaching the doctor. 'Is there any chance we could talk to you, privately, just for a few moments?'

'It'll take more than a few moments to get my

thoughts back!' my mother said. 'Ssssssh,' I said. 'You'll just sound like a crazy woman to the nice doctor here.' My mother looked hurt. 'The doctor hasn't been told it is you yet,' I said, conspiratorially. 'What a handsome man you are, Doctor. Dishy. You've not let me down. You're not a disappointment. But where's your beard?' my mother said.

It was her voice, Mahmud thought. Where had he heard that voice before? 'Excuse me, ladies, but I must get home. I've been feeling a bit under the weather myself recently.'

'It is you, isn't it,' my mother said, agitated. 'I chose . . . oh what's the word? I chose . . .'

'Responsibly!' the doctor said, blurting it out and surprising himself.

'Exactly,' my mother said. 'What is that they say about snowflakes again?' she said.

'That no two snowflakes are exactly the same?' he answered. The doctor stared at my mother and my mother stared at the doctor, looking deeply into each other's eyes as if they'd just discovered a long-lost twin, a familiar. I could almost hear the Mozart that we'd been playing earlier this morning sound in both their heads. 'Did I tell you this is my daughter, Doctor?' my mother was saying. 'I'm Mary,' I said. 'I'm Doctor Mahmud,' he said, shaking my hand. 'What's my name again?' my mother said. 'Nora!' the doctor answered – quick as a flash. 'That's it! Nora, bloody Nora, never liked the bloody name anyway,' my mother said.

'I like it,' the doctor said, smiling. 'Nora's a lovely name. Thank goodness. What would the world be like without Noras?'

The doctor approached the reception. 'I'm going to take this lady through to my surgery. She seems very distressed.'

'I thought you were going home, Doctor?' the receptionist said. The snow was still falling; it would probably lie on top of walls on the way home; there'd be thick snow icing on the roofs of cars; white branches on trees, sparkling roofs, snowy, crunchy secret fields. It was beautiful, the soft, soft snow. The snowflakes were musical notes falling; Mahmud could hear Mozart's piano. 'No. I'm not going home right now. I'm feeling better,' Mahmud said, and smiled enigmatically. 'Through this way, please,' – he took my mother's arm. She was in her element. I could suddenly see her, years back, dancing in the Locarno in that black and white polka-dot dress. 'I chose,' she said to Mahmud again. 'Responsibly,' he repeated, and felt an extraordinary sensation of wonder and calm. 'You chose responsibly.' 'Exactly!' my mother said. Nora was beaming. 'I could dance,' my mother said. 'I could dance and dance and dance.' She was as happy as snowflakes. Her face was flushed; she suddenly looked young again. 'It looks like it is going to lie, the snow,' I said. It was like a fresh sheet of paper, no footprints yet, nothing.

Owl

It was when I was ten and Tawny was nine that we first came across the barn owl on the farmland where our parents went that summer on holiday. We think they went on one last holiday to work out their future, because we heard the four of them whispering often, sometimes furiously. But the noise that stayed with us through our childhood and into our teens was the screech of the barn owl. We gave each other nicknames that night as if to remember, and they stuck well past our forties. I was Barn and she was Tawny. Tawny and Barn. We thought it made us sound like a pair of detectives like Starsky and Hutch, or a pair of comedians like Eric and Ernie. We started dressing in similar clothes. We bought sleuth sweaters. Our parents often took holidays together but this was the first one where we actually noticed that Tawny's father seemed happy chatting to my mother and that my father seemed to laugh in a different way with Tawny's mother.

We always imagined that owls hooted. It was only after that strange holiday on the farm, with the fields and fields of rolled bales of hay and the red tractor and the big jugs of milk fresh from the black-and-white cows and the rows of green, muddy wellington boots outside the porch, and the potatoes that we were allowed to dig up ourselves, that we realized that owls could screech too. And when we got back home and looked up barn owl, we gasped. Tawny said, 'The barn owl is also known as the screech owl,' and I said, 'No!' 'We said it screeched, didn't we!' Tawny said, excited and proud. 'We did. We named it before the encyclopaedia got there!' 'Weird, isn't it,' Tawny said. 'Weirder and weirder,' I said, which was our phrase for everything that was happening around us. We actually saw Tawny's father kiss my mum one night when we'd crept out late to watch the night flights of our barn owl. When we got back into bed breathless and terri-fied, all we could whisper was, 'Weirder and weirder,' and giggle ourselves helplessly to sleep.

'We actually managed to make friends with an owl,' we told our friend when we got back to school. 'How?' Sandra Clark asked, sceptical. 'We brought it things to eat?' 'What things?' she said, her eyes narrowing like her mother's, exactly like her mother's. 'A frog.'

'A frog? I don't believe you!' she said. And for some reason this made her burst into tears. I think she burst into tears because before that summer she had been Tawny's best friend; and Tawny and I returning with new nicknames and tales of our feathered friend made her feel left out. (Well, she wasn't actually there.) 'Two's company, three's a crowd,' we'd always say to the third of the moment, leaving her or me or Tawny alone and miserable for at least a few hours, which felt like days. 'I don't believe you fed a frog to an owl,' Sandra said. 'But why would we lie about something like that?' I said. 'Why lie that you'd fed an owl a frog?'

'So you can say you've done something I haven't,' Sandra said, wiping away her tears.

'That wasn't all we fed the owl,' I continued. Sandra sucked in her cheeks and flicked back her hair. She looked demented. 'What else?' she said, challenging me, her eyes full of hurt and fury. 'We caught a wild rabbit and brought it to our barn owl,' I said. 'Didn't we?' I said to Tawny. Tawny didn't answer. 'Oh, that's just rubbish, just rubbish,' Sandra said and stalked off and Tawny and I split our sides laughing. We couldn't stop. It was painful. 'Sandra's getting so boring,' I said to Tawny and Tawny said 'She's all right,' which made me feel miserable and worried.

'I don't think we should both be called after the owl,' Tawny said to me the next day, 'or else we need a name for Sandra too. Like Feathers or something.'

'But she wasn't there,' I said. 'She never brought the owl a rabbit!' I was outraged. 'You've got to earn your nickname!'

'But *we* never brought the owl a rabbit.'

'But *she's* not to know that!' I said. 'Anyway, we did really because we did it in our head.'

That was when we had a big talk about whether things that happened in your head were real or not: if they could be really real because they happened in your head. I'd already imagined quite a gory and glorious and gut-wrenching scene where our big barn owl gobbles a wild rabbit whole, and it'd hurt me to visualize it so vividly. I'd cried reading *Watership Down*! I'd already kept myself awake at night imagining our barn owl eating a rodent. I'd even just learnt the word rodent in order to say it with complete authority. (I had. I had said to Sandra, 'Did we tell you about the day our owl ate a rodent?' And Sandra had stared aghast and said, 'What's a rodent?' 'A rodent is a rat,' I'd said. I'd been expecting her to ask what a rodent was and I couldn't stop smirking.)

'If you'd known he was such a rat, would you have wasted these years?' That was the question Tawn was asking me now.

'This is what old friends do at our age,' Tawn said, wryly. 'They start going back over their years.'

'Or they sit around and remember their owls,' I said. We both laughed and I somehow managed to avoid the question. Late that afternoon, we drifted off for forty winks. We drifted awake too. It wasn't sudden, but slow. A slow realization that there we were still sitting next to each other, comfortably, after all these years. 'Do you remember Feathers?' Tawn asked me. 'She never knew she was lucky she never saw what we saw.' I wasn't even surprised any more when Tawn and

I thought about the same thing at the same time; we'd been doing that for years. 'I was just remembering her.' I might have even been dreaming her. 'And I was dreaming about that barn owl.'

'Our owl!' Tawn said fondly. 'Our clever owl.'

'What are you going to do?' she asked me.

'Get a place of my own,' I said without a moment's hesitation.

'They say that life begins at forty anyhow!' I said gamely.

'Well, that makes you only ten,' Tawn said laughing. 'And it makes me nine,' she said.

'And there was me waiting to feel grown-up, middle-aged. I still feel like a girl.'

'You still *are* a girl!' Tawn said.

'I thought you said only lesbians stayed girls? And that only heterosexual women grew properly middle-aged?'

'Did I say that?' Tawn said. 'Really? Well then you're not really a proper heterosexual.'

'I'm with a man.'

'Not for much longer!'

'But that doesn't mean I want to be with a woman,' I said. I could feel my hackles rising, like ruffled feathers.

'Do you remember that time when we became convinced we were growing feathers on our arms?' she said, after a brief pause. (Sometimes it seemed Tawn knew me better than I knew myself.)

'Yes, and we thought that soon we'd fly!' I said, swallowing hard.

'And we stood at various parts of the garden and tried to take off?'

'Once I saw my mum kiss your dad.'

'Once I saw my dad kiss your mum.'

It was quite a confusing time. Hard to believe it was forty years ago. I looked at the clock. 'It's late enough now for us to have our gin.'

'Where do you get all these rules from?' Tawn said.

'The middle-aged love rules!' I said. 'They like them more than the young or the old.' I poured us both a gin, chuckling, chucked some ice in and some lime. We always used to like making up untrue facts.

'You'll be fine,' Tawn said. 'You've no idea how free you'll feel.'

'You're on the open road now,' she said. I gulped down my gin. I couldn't imagine my nights. I couldn't think what the nights would be like, locking up downstairs, taking the dog out for the last walk and then locking up, bolting the door.

'You're not going to feel anything like the fear you've been feeling,' Tawn said. 'There's nothing like the fear you feel when you are in the wrong life.'

'How do you know these things?' I asked her.

'Because I'm an owl. You are too.'

'And we were never even in the brownies!' I said.

'Nope nor the . . . what was the other ones called, the ones you could progress to?'

'Can't remember,' I said. 'They wore blue uniforms.'

'It'll come back. This is the kind of thing that happens to forty- and fifty-year-olds even when they are only nine or ten.'

'I know. Scary. Suddenly forgetting things.'

'It's only scary because we all want to be perfect. It's not scary if we just don't care,' Tawn said.

'But it's the feeling of things slipping out of your control, the idea that we might suddenly just lose it, lose our minds.' I could feel a note of hysteria creeping into my voice. I was only half joking.

'We've everything to live for and nothing; that's what you realize when you are forty.'

'That you're at least halfway there?'

'Nope. You realize that you're starting to turn back.'

'Maybe that's why I can't stop thinking about that summer when we found out our mums and dads had swapped.'

'We never talked about it at the time.'

'Do you think it did our heads in?'

'Well, it wasn't exactly calming. It didn't make us feel settled.'

'Do you remember the night of the owl?' Tawn said. I nodded. We hadn't ever talked about that either. Not in excruciating detail. But now that we'd agreed I was ten and she was nine, exactly the ages we were then, it seemed we must. We must face what we saw and what we did about what we saw. And maybe after that we could go back to our names, to calling ourselves our real names. (Though I doubt we'd ever do that. It would sound like we were angry at each other, or suddenly frosty if I out of the blue started calling Tawn Marion and she started calling me Anita. It'd be ridiculous. Our names would sound dated.) 'I could never call you anything other than Tawn,' I said, before we began the frightening work of piecing together the night of the owl. 'Strange, don't you think that we don't really connect our nicknames to the owl any more?'

'After a while, I don't think you connect any name to anything any more. It just is,' Tawn said. She had this way of explaining everything so that everything made perfect sense.

'Do you think you need to drag things up before you can move on?' I asked her. Just thinking about returning was making me feel sick.

'Do you know what?' Tawn said, and her voice sounded elated. 'We don't need to. We don't need to do it. If we don't want to talk about it, we don't have to. Our life has just begun. This is the new one we're in.'

'The past will always try and drag you back,' I said, miserably.

'Not if you don't want it to,' Tawn said. 'Come on, Barn, let's just move on. Let us just do it. Move on. They don't deserve us.'

*

The next morning we both woke up feeling as if we'd released something in the night. 'Shall we go for a walk?' I asked. I didn't want her to leave. We walked to the end of my street and turned left. Then we walked on the meadows for miles. By the Mersey, we saw a heron stand religiously still for some time before taking off, taking flight, its huge wings opening and closing, opening and closing.

The heron reminded me of the wonder we felt as girls watching our owl take off into the starry sky, dive down and come back again, how we soared with it, how we roared when we heard its screech, how our lives felt so up in the air; how, when we imagined something, we became it, effortlessly. 'We had huge wings, didn't we Tawn? I said, a little sadly, the river slow beside me. 'You're starting to sound very middle-aged,' Tawn said. 'Remember you're only ten. And you do still have wings. You're going to need them any time soon.'

The Last of the Smokers

'All my ex-lovers were lovely people: if I can believe that I can give up smoking,' she said. 'Yeah, right,' I said wheezing and laughing. It was past midnight, Saturday night, well, Sunday morning. We were having one of those wild smoking nights. Debbie Murray was practically the only pal left in the whole wide world that still smoked and the one person that could still make me cry with laughter. She pulled out two cigarettes, tapped them both gently, affectionately, on the pack – the way a mother pats a baby's bottom – lit them both at once and handed me one. I took it, smiling.

'I'm serious,' she said, 'dead serious. I've tried every possible other way. Tried the patches, tried the inhalers. In pubs, I'd try and hide the fact that I was sucking that stupid thing, like a five-year-old hiding a dummy. Did I tell you I even tried hypnosis?'

'No way!' I said and laughed so much I brought on a fit of conspiratorial coughing. 'You numpty! What was that like?'

'Mental. And it set me back one hundred and fifty quid which I didn't have,' she said, blowing smoke in my face.

'Which you still don't have,' I said, a little irritated. I'd lent Debbie three hundred smackers last October, which she still hadn't paid back. The idea that she'd burned a hundred and fifty quid on a charlatan hypnotist took the biscuit.

'It was odd. He had a very posh voice and he was trying to frighten me to death. *Your toes are feeling exceptionally heavy. Your legs are very, very heavy. Relax. Think about how filthy your lungs must be . . .* He'd asked for the names of the people I love best in the world. I'd asked if any of them could be dead already and he'd said No, no, no and at that moment I was wondering why not − I mean does he think the dead have no hold over the living? If anything the dead have more hold over the living!' Debbie said. 'True enough,' I said. It was going to be a long night.

'Did you fall into a total trance, then?' I asked, pouring us both a glug of extra wine. 'One more for the road,' I said gamely, knowing that we weren't on a wee country road any more, with badgers hiding behind hedges, no, we were on a big fucking three-lane motorway, midnight juggernauts hurtling down. Debbie inhaled deeply. 'A bit, but just as I was going under I asked him if he had ever sent himself to sleep while hypnotizing someone. He had a lovely voice really. Yes, he said, once, when he was trying to help a petite woman get over her massive panic attacks. He woke to her shaking him roughly back and forth. She was in a total state. That sort of kyboshed it.'

'How long did it work for?'

'Ten days.'

'I hope you went for your money back,' I said with all the authority of my forty-three-year-old self.

'Nah!' Debbie said.

'Why not?' I said, the irritation rising. (Isn't it strange how you can love friends and they can also be horribly maddening?)

'He said it had a ninety-nine per cent success rate. I was ashamed. I didn't want to be the one per cent.'

'Neither did anybody else, probably. What a con. What a rip-off.'

Debbie shrugged her shoulders. She was one of those types that seemed to revel in being ripped off. There was always something grander than money on her mind.

'Anyway, that's all a distraction, Claire,' she said. 'Giving up smoking is a question of belief. If I can substitute one belief for another, right, I might get there. It's not so much that smoking is my crutch. It's that I've got to make giving it up my Church! Need to stop being a martyr, stop seeing it as some sort of sacrifice, right?'

'You're a slaverer,' I said. 'You're a blether of hell.'

'Last time I was at an airport I went into the smoking room, which was right next to the praying room. Then I went into the praying room and prayed I would give up smoking because the smoking room was enough to put you off for life. Smokers don't actually like other people's smoke. It's nasty.'

I inhaled deeply and blew out. I didn't really want Debbie to give up smoking. Nearly everybody I know has given up smoking; even the ones that you would think could never have pulled it off – the thirty-a-day-for-thirty-years diehards. I recited the litany of unexpected names, old friends and lovers who had crossed the border successfully into the non-smoking terrain: Isabel Aird, Adjoa Andoh, Suzanne Batty, Ann Marie Murphy, Pat Milligan, Femi Okafor, Tricia Wood, Ian Jack, Kathryn Perry, Catherine Marcangeli, Brendan Griggs. The list went depressingly on and on. I was starting to feel more and more like I belonged to a tiny band of weirdly devoted people, and every time I ran into a smoker, even a stranger-smoker, I'd light her cigarette gratefully. We were the grateful-not-yet-deads. Perhaps we should all have a special haircut to identify us –the Last of the Smokers, the Last of the Big Pretenders. Debbie got up and put on some John Martyn. I only ever listened to him when I was with Debbie Murray. We blew perfect smoke rings to 'Solid Air'. She tried to sing along, but John Martyn is hard to sing along to. You just sound wrecked.

'You're not very good at picking lovers. You've been with some real lulus,' I said. I could hear my voice was starting to slur.

'Lulus? Christ, where did that come from?'

'Nutters then, bampots and weirdoes!'

'No, they were all lovely! All my ex-lovers were absolutely lovely!' Debbie repeated like a mantra. John

Martyn was singing 'May you never lay your head down without a hand to hold, and may you never lay your body out in the cold.' Debbie sang along to that bit, quite fiercely. 'The only person in my life who has lasted is you,' Debbie said, at the end of the song, sadly. 'Maybe friends are the big loves of your life. Maybe we get it all wrong, focusing on lovers like we do.'

'We ask too much of lovers,' I agreed.

'Like hell we do! We don't ask *enough*!' Debbie said. She had reached the point where she might start to turn.

'I think we should get to bed. It's late. It's one in the morning.'

'We've got to sort this out,' Debbie said. 'This is important. If we sort this out right now, tonight, by tomorrow we could be non-smokers. Think of it! We could be free! Think how wonderful it would be to say *I don't smoke.* What a beautiful fucking sentence!'

'We'll never be non-smokers,' I said. 'The most we can hope for is being ex-smokers. It never even occurred to the non-smoker to smoke. They just don't get it.'

'Don't be smart!' Debbie said and went to light up two again at the same time. 'You're all right,' I said. 'I don't want one right now.' I felt a moment's lovely superiority. Debbie looked fazed, then dazed, then lit up regardless, trying to appear debonair. Joni was singing now, 'The last time I saw Richard was in Detroit in '68, and he told me all romantics meet the same fate some day . . .'

'So that's the secret,' Debbie said, leaning forward, excitedly. 'Ex-lovers and ex-smokers. We have to do a switch.'

'You've lost me,' I said.

'Concentrate!' she said. 'I'm on to something!' She swallowed the last swirl of wine. 'Open another bottle to go with this! This is electrifying!'

'No, it's too late to open another bottle,' I said.

I was starting to wonder about her theory, actually. It's impossible for me to become someone who has never smoked. It is impossible for me to become someone who has never loved. I will not ever become a non-lover. I have accumulated exes. These days I read the zodiacs of three major exes to see if they are having any luck. The full moon this Wednesday forecasts major changes for all my ex-lovers. I gave in and opened a screw-top called Laid Back Ruby to help me work out Debbie Murray's Fantastically Complicated Way to Give up Smoking.

I am lover-less at the moment; so is Debbie. We've both been like that for two years. If one of us gets a lover the other will find it tricky, but not as tricky maybe as if one of us gives up smoking. We've been smoking together for nearly thirty years. I remember our first Sobranie. Our pal Gillian Baxter's parents gave us one each on New Year. Her mother held open a beautiful Black Russian box. I picked a pink Sobranie;

Debbie picked a blue. We both had an Advocaat and lemonade. We were fourteen, sophisticated, cool, already inhaling. That New Year Debbie sang along to Gilbert O'Sullivan singing 'Claire'. She liked that there was a song with my name in it. I remember smoking our first Consulate and Debbie saying, It's no worse really than sucking a Polo mint then she blew a smoke ring.

If she gives up and I don't, I'll regard it as a huge betrayal, worse even than her stealing a girlfriend. Debbie's last bloke was a moron. Then she had a girl, Lucky, well she called her Lucky because she gambled all the time, but actually she was very unlucky and she blew all Debbie's savings. She never really liked any of my lovers either when I think about it.

I've lived through two lesbian dictatorships: one of them even had a tiny moustache. For some reason, I've always been drawn to people stronger than me, to obsessive types. The first of the lesbian dictators had a big thing about cats. In fact, she first fell for me because one of her Refuge cats sat on my lap. 'That's very unusual,' she said, her eyes widening with excitement. 'Mrs MacDonald is usually very, very fussy about who she sits on.' 'Is that right?' I said. I wished her cats weren't called such stupid names. 'Yes, I've no idea what happened to her before she came to me, but somebody abused her. You can tell an animal's past.' Then she leant towards me and kissed me on the lips. It took me aback. When I did that thing, you know, replaying what had happened to try and give some pleasure, that line about the animal past always stuck and stopped me going further. It was as irritating as static.

She was called Caroline, the Cat Woman, and she was very beautiful really. She had a haughty intelligence that you could detect around her cheekbones that was quite cat-like. She was enigmatic, never gave much away. I never met any of her family and she never spoke of them at all. She enjoyed listening to me talking about my family. She loved my imitations of my mother and father. Her face would grow furry with pleasure. She even kept a cat-journal. The last straw for me was when we came back from Florence. 'Mrs MacDonald is sulking because we've been away,' Caroline wrote in the journal. 'Not even Michelangelo's *David* was worth it. I've put Mrs MacDonald back months, just as she was starting to trust me. That's it – no more holidays!' I read that with growing alarm.

'Smoking is my first erotic memory, when I think about it,' Debbie was saying. We were so drunk by now that we were more or less talking or thinking to ourselves. We'd returned to the state of the quintessential smoker, a luxurious state of aloneness. I took my fag out and stood at the back door and smoked under the sizzling, smoky stars. I would miss the starry-smoke the most. What is the point in having a gorgeous night sky without a cigarette to go with it? Just thinking about stopping was making me feel nostalgic. I went back in. Debbie was stuck on the same sentence. 'Yes,' she was saying, as Joni sang. 'Yes, smoking is erotic.' She stubbed her fag out. The ashtray was overflowing. It was filthy, actually. Filthy, dirty. How any of us could do it was beyond me. Every time I managed to give up, I stared with horror at those that still smoked. How can they do it, how can they, I'd think, in the twenty-first century, knowing all that we know? I'd stare at the woman puffing away waiting for a bus, at the widower with his widower's shopping in one hand and his fag in the other, at the clutch of teenage girls inhaling and exhaling nonchalantly, and I'd think, you're crazy, crazy, crazy, you're going to die! Picture the oxygen tent! And then three weeks or nine months or one year later, I'd be back with them again. Unbelievable! Apart from anything else, it looks deeply weird, smoking, like something human beings were never supposed to do. Unnatural, all that smoke coming out the nose and the mouth.

'Do you remember your first kiss,' Debbie said, 'your first long snog? I remember mine. It was under a desk. Kenny Davies stuck his tongue in my mouth and then slid his lips across like two wee grass snakes or something. It wasn't very pleasant.'

'Yuck,' I said.

'Slippy, slithery, sneaky. See. That's another similarity between smoking and sex. The first time, both stink. The first fag is a nauseating experience, right? It gives you the boke. I remember Margaret Morton forcing me to inhale so I could be one of the gang. It was horrible. Really-really-really. Not nice. Not pleasant. I remember thinking there's no way I'm ever going to get addicted, but I smoked on and off, and off and on, and I'd say to myself I'm not addicted, right?'

Debbie was looking traumatized now. The thought of giving up completely was doing her head in. I know. It was like facing the abyss, the well of loneliness. No companion, there. What was there? It was like a big dark void or something. I poured us both another glass of wine. My watch said three a.m. 'You still thinking we should give up tonight?' I said. 'What about tomorrow? Tonight's not the best night.'

'Don't play games with me!' Debbie said snarling in my face. 'It will always win. You can't bargain. It will always get you. The only way is to make them lovely people. What did they give me – the ex-lovers. The buzz? They gave me a hit, an excitement, right, and I thought I couldn't sleep without them, right, and that I would get terrible mood swings if I gave them up, and that I wasn't capable of being sociable on my own.'

'Are you talking about lovers or cigarettes?' I asked.

'Same difference. Actually the cigarettes, they understood me better than the lovers. A cigarette is an enigmatic lover who understands all your intricate complexities without you having to say a single word or have a word said back,' Debbie said. She was one of those people that could actually sound quite pompous drunk. It was loveable really.

'I see,' I said. Well, I did.

I was back on my own again thinking about the lover that came after Caroline, the Cat Woman. She was another right warmer. Fiona. She was very judge-mental and had absolutely no sense of humour. But she was a mixture because she was sentimental too. On the day we met the juke box was playing that song – who sang it? – she's got Bette Davis eyes. A smoky voice, remember? It was romantic. Fiona smoked back in those smoking days. But then she suddenly and violently changed, joining the vicious band of ex-smokers, who believe that smoking is evil like a new wacky religion. I remember the day she gave up; she said, very snootily, 'Once you decide, it's easy. You just have to choose your moment. Actually,' she said, even more snootily, *the moment chooses you!*' That day she took the curtains to the dry-cleaners and hired one of those shampoo-the-carpet jobs. She sniffed the air. She painted the living-room walls magnolia. Fresh start, she said. You too. I pretended to give up, but any opportunity I got I sneaked a fag and then sucked extra-strong mints all the way home. I'd get in, run up the stairs, wash my hands, spray perfume all over, until one time she caught the hint of something on my breath and said that she couldn't trust me any more. If I was going behind her back to smoke in secret, I could

just as easily have an affair. She asked me to choose, the
fags or her. I chose the fags, packed my bags and I was
out of there in a week. No love lost really. I fell upon
my pack of cigarettes and upped my daily intake.

'It's all about desire,' Debbie was saying as I rum-
maged in the cupboard for something else to drink.
I found an old bottle of tequila. Well, the sun was
rising. We'd moved on to Neil Young now. He was
singing in his heartbreaking beautiful voice, *I've seen
the needle and the damage done, a little part of it in every
one, but every junkie's like a setting sun.* 'One last nip
for the road,' I said warningly. I tried to visualize a
Junction 7 exit on our motorway. 'Yep,' she said. She
was nearly passing out now anyway. 'Did you ever
desire me?' 'No, don't be daft,' I said shocked and a bit
wary. 'Why not?' she said, genuinely curious. 'Why not
when you are a lesbian.'

'You're my mate,' I said. 'And you're like my sister.
It would be like incest or something.'

Debbie smiled. This answer seemed to please her.
'Well, I never desired you either. I desired to smoke. I
desired my cigarettes. For them, I had too much desire,'
she said grandly, putting on an Edith Piaf accent.

'There was a while when I craved a lover,' I said,
'but that's gone now. Don't even feel a pang of regret.
Well rid. That's what I think. I got well rid.'

'That's not the right attitude,' Debbie said, sounding suddenly sober. She could do this: suddenly turn

sober. It was very fucking freaky. Like somebody going BOO! 'The correct attitude is to find a way to make them lovely in your memory. Give them the nostalgia!' she said triumphantly, like she had suddenly found the key. 'Give them the nostalgia!' she repeated, her voice deepening. 'GIVE THEM THE NOSTALGIA!' she said, this time sounding very crude.

'I'll tell you what, Debs,' I said. 'If all I've got to do at the end of this head-fuck night from hell is give up smoking, it's going to be quite easy. My ex-lovers had nice things about them, yes. The Cat Woman loved her cats. She was nice to her friends. She got upset at tsunamis and disasters. She gave money to charity. She donated her blood regularly. She visited a lonely old neighbour every Sunday afternoon and took her a little cake, an Eccles cake.'

'Really?' Debbie swung around and stared at me, definitely stone-cold sober now. 'You never told me any of this? How come you never told me any of this?'

'It was more fun slagging her off, like it was more fun smoking,' I said, putting out my last doubt ever, squashing it into the ashtray with a new, fresh deter-minedness.

Debbie lit up again, God, she must have smoked twenty-five, at least! The room was thick with fug. I opened the window. 'Let it out,' I said. 'Tomorrow, I'm going to take the curtains to the cleaners.' 'You what?' Debbie said. She looked disappointed in me, like she wasn't expecting to be taken seriously. 'I'm through with smoking,' I said flashily. 'Smoking is so last year.'

'I hate it when people use the word *so* like that,' Debbie said morosely.

'Smoking is common,' I said, ignoring this, 'we've got to get out before we're the last ones left on the planet who smoke. Let's join the other gang. They're the cool ones now.'

Debbie cupped her hands around her fag. She looked so lonely. I felt sorry for her, but I had my health to consider. I had my lungs to think about, my blood circulation. 'Listen,' Debbie said, taking a deep drag, miffed, 'this was my idea.'

'I know,' I said, 'but it's going to be a tough one for you, because your ex-lovers were psychopaths. Mine were all quite nice people really.'

'You think that because it was you that left them. None of them left you,' Debbie said, lighting up yet another filthy cigarette.

'True, true,' I said evenly.

'I'm always the one that's left,' Debbie said, and suddenly shocked me by bawling her eyes out. 'Put the fag out,' I said, 'and come and look at the sun coming up. It is bright red.' We stood outside my back door, linking arms looking at the red eye of the rising sun for a long, long time. Debbie didn't light up. Maybe Debbie would never light up. Maybe we would both become very boring. 'I think we're going to become boring people,' Debbie said with that uncanny ability to speak my inside thoughts aloud. 'Shut up, baby,' I said in my best *Double Indemnity* voice. 'Let's get some shut-eye. It's late.' The morning clouds were swirling in the sky, like wee puffs of smoke.

Mini Me

Day One

See every time I goes on a diet, I remember all they diets that have gone afore: like auld illnesses, they come wey memories o' intense sadness. This time it's going tae work; I'm telling you why. It's working because ma dedication is *up there*, optimum, second to none. I've tested masell and ma answers are all *aye*. I'm aw across it.

I tried not to get too *doon* this morning when I got oot the auld exercise bra frae the previous diet and wis shocked to find ma knockers didnae fit intae it. So furst up, and as a matter o' urgency, I hud to heave myself to the sports shop. I says to the girl you should be ashamed o' yoursell! You're supposed to be supporting people tae get healthy and there you ur discriminating – no support for ower 36 DD! And I says, *it's a scandal.* The girl looks at me like she despises me when she doesnae even know me and she's saying on repeat *no my problem, no my problem.* And I says *what's the matter are you on a low vocab diet?* And she clamps her mooth shut, folds her airms and stares, just stares, cool as you like, cool as the bloody cucumbers I'm having tae masticate. So I just hud tae leave the sporty shop, waddle oot wey as much dignity as I kid muster. I hears her shout after me *sort your head out, weirdo!* but I resisted the urge tae go back and have it out wey her. I've mair tae worry aboot than ratty lassies in retail therapy.

Next up: I tries Marks for support, and finds a nice wuman who has a whiff o' lez aboot her and appears tae enjoy taking ma measurements. I leave Marks at two with the bra in ma bag, black and stretchy. (It won't be too lang till I get back intae the auld sports bra; this wan is a wee go-between.) But then ma tummy rumbles; shopping is pure knackering! I'm no meaning to be funny but even going up the escalator tires me oot! (I'm scared o' them; huv to hit that first step hopping.) Am gonnae huv tae start this diet the morrow – I'm pure starving now what with having tae go in search o' a boulder-holder and a' I had fir breakfast wis a pink grapefruit which has no exactly put a lining in ma stomach. It felt mair like it took the lining aff my stomach! They say that coffee and tea are negative waters; well, the grapefruit is a negative fruit. So I goes and has masell a *caffe latte*, the skimmed milk is mair *fattening* if yir on a diet, so I believe – this is the conundrum – and an almond croissant. They don't even pretend to have skinny almond croissants. Though they do huv skinny muffins – I mean, *please!* You might as well stick some blueberries into an empty egg carton and have done wey it.

Day One

I didnae bother recording ma intimate thoughts fir the rest o' yesterday; I reckoned it couldnie coont as a dieting day. But today is Tuesday and furst things furst – the scales! I'm noo heavier than I wis yesterday morning due to the croissants, the big Mac (which I boycotted fir ages because my surname is MacDonald), the spag bol, the deep-fried Mars bar, the Chinese cairrie oot, the bumper bag of crisps. Wis a bit sickened. I've got to the stage where I look at masell in the mirror and say *how did you let yoursell go?* But ah canny be hanging aroond asking existential questions – is the self something that kin be let go and if so kin you still be staunding? – got tae keep up the momentum, and be true to ma vision when I started this brand-new diet. I kid see masell slim! That's what I huv tae do when I'm trying to shed stones, I huv tae carry a mini *me* inside ma mind's eye, a wee me. I gie masell the figure o' Michelle Obama. To look like her I have tae gie masell some extra inches in height. It's do-able: getting fit makes ye taller tae. I huvtae believe she's possible, this *mini me*, like I've got something invested in her materializing. And before she's even here, what you huvtae say is *this is it* this time, you're gonnae hang

on tae her? You are no gonnae let her go. Right? It's
not getting the weight doon that's the problem: it's the
third wumun that comes alang when you've reached yer
goal, trying to wreak havoc. It's the third wumun I'm
ready for when she saunters up and jist starts adding
things, slowly, creepily, a wee scone here, a wee tattie
there, a wee tattie scone, a toty knob of butter. I'm
keeping an eye oot for her. I'm intae this diary so I kin
chart and maintain the loss.

Aye, diets are mair like bereavements. What happens tae me when I shed a shitload o' stones is that I
feel sad for the auld fat girl who used tae stare sadly
intae the mirror trying tae day something wey hersell,
the wan who turned hauf aroond in the mirror to grab
haud o' her back fat, and subconsciously, mibbe, bring
her back. Truth is: I'm a bit o' an alien when I'm
skinny; I don't recognize masell – suddenly auld, suddenly miserable-looking. At least I look happy fat. At
least you can still look young when yer overweight,
a wee bit o' the cherub in yer cheeks. So that's the
other thing aboot this time. I'm going tae huv a wee
ceremony fir the auld fat me, jist like I wid if I'd
died and this time I'm going to bag up her claes and
put some intae Oxfam, some intae Red Cross and some
intae the Elderly Care, so I'm really, truly spreading
masell thin! (The fat claes are all like funeral claes
anyway – aw black.) But I'm no there yet. I'm on DAY
ONE which should really be DAY TWO but I'm not
goin tae judge. (That's the other thing: get rid o' the

judgemental voice inside yer ain heid!) This time a'
the claes are going, the minute they're loose, I'm getting well rid. (I canny wait for that. Canny wait to
put my haunds doon my expanding-waist troosers, pull
them way oot and say to Iain, look how much I've lost.)
It's all aboot how much you've lost. That's how you
define a weight-watcher: loss. It's a' aboot loss; everything's a' aboot loss. The time before the last time when
I actually joined WeightWatchers, I used to quite look
forward to the weigh-in! Aye! If Sandra said, 'Good for
you, Patricia, you've lost four pounds,' it wis better
than a night oot at the bingo. But WeightWatchers is
nae the answer. They say things like GOOD NEWS:
THIS WEEK YOU CAN HAVE A BOWL OF COCO
POPS! I mean, c'mon! You're supposed to wet yoursell
wey excitement, the *wow* factor o' a bowl o' Coco Pops!
C'mon!

Back to the claes: I'm never again goin tae sneakily
keep them in a suitcase under ma bed for the return
o' the big lassie. No way! Nor am I going back tae the
charity shops hunting aroon fir ma auld claes, telling
masell I'm double donating tae console, that disnae
work either! It disnae work and it reduces morale.
That's whit the dieter needs mair than anything:
morale. It's a hard thing to nail on day one, I'm telling you; yer self-esteem is shot tae pieces. And who are
you gonnae blame? A' the snooty-nosed people that
look doon at you, sneakily eyeing yer midriff. A' the
people that talk to you like yer stupit, when yer no

stupit, like yer brain's slow cos yer walk's slow. All the skinny judgementals; they're the disturbed ones. Tell you why. Because they canny take their eyes aff ma fat arse, that's why!

Day One

Yesterday wisnae as successful as I hoped cos an auld pal called roon unannounced and asked me oot fir an *all ye can eat* Chinese buffet. I telt her I was trying to watch ma weight (a weird phrase; yer weight is no the telly) so we compromised and settled on a curry; she'd jist lost her ma so I couldnie refuse and I couldnie say whit I wanted tae say which wis curries are killers fir me and I couldnae jist order the chicken wey no rice because it wid have made her feel lonely. So frae no fault o' my own, I told masell I'd have to postpone the diet and try an keep up the momentum as best I kin. Actually, the curry in the Coriander was so tasty, perhaps the best curry o' my entire life, and Jenny had Chicken Tikka Masala and I had Grandma's Beef and we both shared a pilau rice and a peshwari nan. That would have been fine but Jenny canny go fir a curry weyoot ordering an onion bhaji, so I kept her company. Ditto the spicy popadoms, spicy onions and mango chutney, vegetable samosa and aloo papa chat. You canny go oot wey a pal and let them eat starters on their ain; it's no right, am I right or am a meringue? This is where all this dieting goes pear-shaped so it does; it doesnae allow you tae huv any manners. Yer sitting in a pal's hoose, and yer saying *I'm not eating carbs at the moment* when they've gone to the big bother of making a homemade lasagna? No carbs fir me – when they've dug up new potatoes from their back gairden? It's no do-able. Hauf way through the meal wey Jenny, I suddenly remembers that the last time I properly dieted (because I am going to properly start tomorrow) the time when I lost four and a hauf stone, six years ago noo, I hud tae become very anti-social. It's the only way, lock yoursell in at night and don't see any mates. Don't travel. Don't go anywhere! The minute you do, yer resolve will crack. Take yoursell pumpkin seeds intae work, if you've gotta work, keep the heid doon, and make yersell a salad. It's a regime all right. *Think positive!* Jenny asks me last night how me and Iain are getting on. I says, Fine, ok. Jenny says, Sure? I says, he's a bit undermining o' me dieting, like he's an agent saboteur. And Jenny says, dipping her nan into her sauce, Are you dieting, you could of fooled me! (She disnae believe me; but I'll show her. The proof is in the pudding. Or rather the proof is in no pudding.) I says, Yip, I'm starting the morrow. Jenny groans. Jenny is no lightweight hersell. Yeah, Iain says to me, Pat, yo-yo dieting doesnie wurk. And what did you say? Jenny says.

I says, It's six years since I've been on a diet, you'd hardly call that a bloody yo-yo. And I says, It'd have to be some yo-yo that takes six years fir tae pull the bloody string back up! Jenny pisses herself laughing. He might like you the way you are, Jenny says, knocking back her pint of Cobra. True, I says, a lot o' men like their wives on the generous side, eh no? Whit is *that* aboot?

Day One

I've decided that I'm no mentally prepared for the regime and the strange lonely weeks ahead, I've other things going aff this week, and emotionally it's no been easy listening to Jenny talking aboot the death o' her maw; it's triggered aff things for me, things I thought I wis ower. So I've made an executive decision tae start the diet properly NEXT Monday. It's a bit o' a heidbanger anyway trying to start a diet in the middle o' the week. You don't know where you are and you get lost trying to count things. Dieting is maths. I've never been all that brilliant wey counting. Not that I'm blaming my weight on no being good at mental arithmetic, but it disnae help. Think aboot it! I weigh sixteen and a half stone and I want to lose four stone minimum; minimum. MINIMUM FOR MINI ME! That's adding and subtraction. The diet I'm on the noo promises I'll lose twelve pounds in seventeen days. So that's a pound and a half a day. If on day two I lose three pounds, how am I supposed to work it all oot? That's maths too. BUMS MEAN SUMS! And there's the weighing oot o' foods that's a pain in the arse. And there's the drinking eight glesses o' water. That's the most difficult part. I canny hack it. And yer on gless three and yer asking yerself is this my third or ma fourth gless o' water? Ye really can't remember. So you knock back another jist in case and nearly gie yerself the boke. Still I'm going to have to embrace all that again if I want tae turn masell aroond. And I do. Aw, I really do. I really, really want tae turn masell roond. I want a whole new figure. See even the word for that is connected wey numbers! It's a maths mafia dieting is, so it is. Aye. *Go Figure!* They say that in the States don't they, where they have people much bigger than me. *Go Figure.* I don't know why I hate the expression, but I do. Some of those people over there are stuffing their faces with donuts all day lang.

Day One

I've given myself a good talking to and am ready to commence on my seventeen-day diet. It will slice the first stone aff me in nae time, that bit is pure plain sailing. I'm not seeing any pals fir two weeks. I'm going tae go into work and straight home to Iain, no drinks doon the pub. No rounds. Should save masell a fortune! I'm going tae be fifty this year, and I've dieted hauf my life away. Aye well: nae mair, nae mair same auld same auld. Nae mair yo-yo. Nae Mair Atkins; nae mair Hay. This wan is the vanishing trick!

So first up: The Scales! The scary sadist supercilious scales. They wait an agonizing minute before they break the news. Bastards. I'm five pounds heavier than I wis last Monday, I shouldnie have hud that bloody curry, but let's no get doon-hearted; excess will be gone in the wink o' an eye. I get in the shower: huv a good wash in freezing-cold water, kick-start ma circulation. Brrrrrrrr! No nice. I huv an inspirational idea: I clip my pubic hair! I stand shivering wey the scissors hinging between my fleshy thighs. Phew. Snip, snip. That makes me feel hauf a pound lighter awready! I waddle doon tae the kitchen in ma buff and squeeze hauf a lemon into a gless and add water. But I suddenly remember that I huv a bottle of tree syrup in the fridge from when I wis going to start *the lemon detox diet* but didnae. I'm sure me combining diets willnae do any hairm. I pour masell a plentiful helping o' tree syrup. I add a pinch of cayenne which is supposed tae speed up yer metabolism. *Woo Hoo! I'm awa!* It really is day one and I'm losing it. I'm really going tae lose it. I slice a ruby grapefruit in hauf and put it on a white plate. The grapefruit and the lemon huv got ma digestive juices going that's fir sure. I can feel them dancing. I put on Aretha and move to *Say A Little Prayer*. I sing along: *the moment I wake up before I put on my makeup*. When I gets to the bit about wondering what dress to wear, I realize that I huvnie worn a dress since I was twenty.

Sometime in the afternoon, I realizes I made a miscalculation with numbers. If I'm tae lose twelve pounds in seventeen days that is less than a pound a day. I have tae put seventeen intae twelve no the other way aroon. I don't even know whit that is or whether it's gonnae show on the scales. How am I going tae know if I lose a bit of a pound? Cannae dwell on that. Have to get oot and walk fast for seventeen minutes. Even though I can feel it's putting pressure on ma knees. What I'm thinking is imagine strapping into a seat on an airplane and not having tae adjust the seatbelt? What I'm thinking is imagine all the compliments that are gonnae be coming ma way. Naebody bothers to gie you a compliment when yer fat. Everybody looks doon on you like yer some kind of monster. You can hear their inside thoughts when they're looking at you, even yer ain family. You can hear them thinking, *Look at the state of that. She's huge. She's massive. The size of her! What a strain on her heart.* All of it, you can hear the whole lot.

Goal: to lose four and a hauf stone. To tune intae my hunger meter. To eat like a skinny person. Pay attention tae the way they eat next time yer oot. Watch their trolleys in the supermarkets. Learn to *spy* on skinny people! Goal: to put on the skinny claes still optimistically hinging in the wardrobe. To cut my toenails weyoot getting oot o' breath; to see my pubic hair when I'm lying doon in the bath. That's when I'll know my stomach is flat.

When I got in from work last night, Iain was tucking into a big bowl of left-over spag bol. I found myself feeling a bit disgusted. (And worse, I found myself feeling a bit superior because I'd eaten nothing but rocket and pricey balsamic vinegar all day.) Wan thing: I'd forgotten how quickly the exhilaration kicks in. I'm going tae do this. It's no because I want people to find me attractive; it's jist because I want people to *find me*. (But also fir my health, but.)

Day Two

Got up early and couldnae wait to get on The Scales then remembered that sleeping burns yer fat so went back to bed for a bit. Called in sick. (You canny be expected to diet seriously *and* go into work.) Wis a bit thirsty but didnae want to sip the water next to my bed in case that appeared on *The Scales.* So I goes back to bed for a snooze, but I've started feeling very anxious and am breaking oot in sweats. Before too lang, I had conked oot, phew! Gets up again, two hours later with a pounding head. I stands on The Scales and takes a deep breath like I'm facing my primary school headmaster. But I needn't have worried. It's all good. Doon three pounds. *Get in! Go figure!*

Canny wait till I get below fifteen stone, then I'll start to feel like I'm on safe ground. Below fourteen, I'll feel like I'm going places. Below thirteen, the ground will move under my feet and I'll dance to that song. *See the earth move under my feet. See the sky come tumbling down, tumbling down.* Below twelve, might as well be on hallowed ground. I might take up meditation because by that time I'll be able tae cross my legs, hopefully. Below eleven, I've never ever been (well not since I was a wee girl anyway, and that is another lifetime away) but I imagine it must feel like shifting sand, and the third girl is already standing there, licking her big fat ice-cream cone. No worries, I'm getting ahead of myself; the wan I'm going to be shortly. Say four months max. It's not a lot, is it, to change yer life – four months?

Just had a big salad for lunch, tinned tuna in brine, boiled eggs, leaves, tomatoes, green beans, bit of olive oil since it is counted as good oil, squeeze of lemon. Where's the hardship in that? The wan hardship is it is costing me mair money, a' this organic stuff. It's way mair expensive. Never mind, wance I shed the skins, they'll be less o' me to feed and I'll save pounds. *Save pounds shedding pounds*, that's my logo when I run this diet and puts masell forward for *The Apprentice*.

I am just not feeling hungry. *I am just not feeling hungry!* It's easy no tae slip wance you are in the zone. When you're in the zone, nothing can stop you! You have to play tricks on your body. (I know that sounds sexual, it's not.) What you huv to do is trick your body into burning fat. Aye! You have to not let it get complacent. Jist when yer enjoying yer egg-white omelette, when you've got yer heid aroond that one, it's time to eat *sashimi*! You have to see yer body as yer adversary so you can trick it properly. Reduce yer carbs so yer body taps intae storage fat. Increase proteins so yer body goes into fat-burning mode. Is burning your

own fat more eco-friendly or not? Is it better for the
environment? These are fat philosophical questions.

But later, when I'm putting my breasts intae ma
sports bra, I suddenly feels a bit of affection for them and
gies them a little pat. Why should I no be kind tae you
I find masell saying later, wey a gless o wine or two doon
me. The hubbie wis oot for the coont on the armchair.

It's all psychology, dieting; you'd be amazed. When
I goes out fir my fast walk, the sweat wis pouring
between ma breasts so I reckoned I was walking fast
enough. It said in ma book keep yer back straight, yet
tummy tight and squeeze yer buttocks when ye walk
fast. I tried that and nearly put ma back oot. So I'm
jist sticking tae walking fast. I canny even locate my
buttocks tae be honest. Anyhow, I jist kept repeating
to myself like a mantra. You're going to do it. You're
going to beat this sack of cement.

Day Three

I can't believe I'm actually excited about my date wey
The Scales. I took ma earrings aff, didnae want them
adding anything. Today I was doon another three! Even
my mental arithmetic is getting better! So that's six
pounds already and I'm only supposed to lose twelve
pounds for the whole seventeen days, so that means
I just need to stay on it for another two days and job
done! Then I can go on to the next cycle. Joke! I'm not
trying to get oot noo. No mair excuses! I do not even

have to persuade myself to steer clear o' mashed tatties. I remarked upon this to Iain tonight. And he said, 'Is that all you can talk aboot, this bloody diet? You're starting to bore the arse aff me. You've become the tattie bore.' He laughed to himself. I looked at him. He was stuffing his face with a kebab. I thought to myself, *Suit yourself: your days are numbered, mate.* And I suddenly realized why Jenny asked me that question.

I went oot to take an early evening fast walk around ma block. Three times round my block, I thought. No bother. So I'm walking fast as I can manage and somebody comes up to me and says, 'Excuse me? Have you got the time on you?' I jist kept walking fast as I could till I could feel the sweat on ma fore heid. As if I could stop to look at my watch! Some people are so selfish!

Day One

Got side-tracked just when I wis doing so well. You can never tell when things are gonna come at ye fray the left field. Started this morning again wey a squeezed lemon and felt my eyes well up fir nae good reason. In the shower, I got hold o a ring o' my fat and decides tae talk directly tae it. I says, Yer finished, yer over, you're so . . . and I searched for the right word and found it – auld-fashioned. That's what ye are. *Auld-fashioned!* All the trendy fifty-year-olds are fit. Yer no fit. Yer a disgrace. Yer a complete disgrace. Whit would yer mammy say if she wis still alive, dae ye think? Eh?

She'd say, Pat, you're fat; you've put the beef on. You'll need to get rid of it, Patricia MacDonald. I'm telling you. Strangely, my maw wis a wee skinny woman so I canny blame a fat gene. Whit can I blame? I canny think o' any particular time in ma childhood that's led to this.

When I looks up at ma face in the mirror, I'm greeting. Good, I says tae masell. Well – good. Cry like a big wean and get yersell sorted oot! I can think of other diets that have begun in tears. In point o' fact, all the successful diets have begun in tears. And Iain's no here any mair tae chip in or undermine me. He's aff wey the lassie frae his office. I know! Whit a cliché. You'd think he'd be tae embarrassed tae carry it oot; but naw, naebody, it seems, is tae embarrassed tae carry oot a cliché.

Day One

Last week wis a write off, right. I've written it aff. I wisnae in the right frame o' mind. I was aff my heid. Losing it. The wan thing that cheered me up wis that I read in a magazine that red wine burns off fat. So I've got myself a bottle tae glug the night. *Organic red* – no jist any rubbish.

Day One

It wis a waste of time, that red wine. I didnae come doon in weight at all. It didnae help mibbe that I drunk the whole bottle. It tells you jist to have a gless. But who do you know who can jist have a gless? I'm having nothing come at me frae the left field. I've had to go sick again because it's starting to stress me oot, ma own fat face in the mirror. I says to masell, Do you know whit you are? Yer *morbidly obese*, that's whit you are. Do you know why they use the word morbid? Because yer going to die! You are going to die if you carry on like this. Yer heart will jist give oot. Or you'll have a stroke. Or you'll jist drap doon deid. It's up tae you, I says. Do you want to be *morbidly obese?* So. It starts right here, right now. Fir my breakfast I had a hauf o' a pink grapefruit and a boiled egg, no toast no butter. For my lunch I had a whole cucumber and six tomatoes and a cup of green tea, which is a fat-burner too. For my dinner I had a chicken leg and a bit of broccoli. (I added a tiny knob of butter.) And another bottle of red wine. Iain phoned in the middle of my meagre meal but I let him piss off straight to answerphone. I got up and hovered by it and listened.

I could hear him saying, 'Pat, this is a pattern, can ye no see that, hen? You push me away when you're on a diet. It's like ye have to shed me. Nae wonner I have to look elsewhere for comfort. Gie me a call back. Miss you.' The phone goes dead. He sounds sloshed. I turn the volume doon. So it's ma fault, again. All ma fault. I goes straight up and intae my bed. I put the telly on and watch *Desperate Housewives*. It's no that funny any mair; it's stretching it a bit, and those housewives arenie nearly as desperate as me. And that voiceover at the beginning is getting on my nerves. But I wouldnie mind having Bree's figure. I toss and turn, must be the bloody caffeine in that green tea that's keeping me awake. It's no real. It's no real so it's no.

Day Two

Had a night of well weird dreams. Woke up and staggered to the scales. Doon two. Aha. I felt my stomach, definitely getting noticeably smaller. Looking forward to having just one ring round my stomach, like the rubber ring I used to wear when I was learning to swim. Then looking forward to having no rubber ring at a'. Iain's away a while noo. Do I miss him? Naw. But it's weird but the way your whole life suddenly seems a bit o' a con. Like everybody wis pretending everything. What I've concluded is naebody knows naebody knows naebody. Do you know what I mean? Yiv had a stranger in yer ain bed for twenty-odd years.

Last night I got oot the photie albums. Fat in that wan. Fat in that wan. Fat in that wan. I shut the book, screwed off. I couldnie see what I ever saw in Iain or what he ever saw in me. I kept hearing him say yer mine for life. But like I say, it wis me that instigated a' this. Iain liked me big because his mammy wis big and he was breastfed. (I didnae like the amount of attention he showered on my breasts anyway. It did nothing fir me. *Nothing fir me!*) Naw, seriously. And he kept saying,

You're no yersell when you've lost a' that weight. You look odd. Other women's husbands would be egging them on. I don't seem to do much of an evening except write oot my recipes for the next day and plan ma day aroond them. Iain was right. I've turned into a tattie bore.

Day One Hundred and Forty-Three

Bingo! Doon three pounds in the wan go! Wis getting worried there because I'd reached a plateau and I thought I wisnae going to go any lower. But noo, here I am. Bang on twelve stone. Jist wan more stone to go. See this dieting it takes ye through a rollercoaster o' emotions, so it does. One minute you're high cos you're shedding and the next minute you're low cos you're piling it back on. Focus, Patricia MacDonald! Stay focused. Fir ma brekkie I had a yoghurt and some raspberries. For ma lunch I had an omelette jist wey egg whites, and it wis OK. For ma dinner I had a chicken leg and a bit of broccoli with a friendly knob o' butter. At aboot seven that night, Jenny calls me and asks me oot. 'I haven't seen you for ages,' Jenny says. I put on the jeans that have been hanging in my wardrobe unworn for six years, and top, ditto. Slashes on a bit of lippy.

So we go doon to the local, the Horse and Jockey, and it's a bit bonkers in there cos there's a pub quiz going on. So we leave and go the other pub across the road where Jenny stares at me fir ages. She doesnie look at me like the people at work do and say you're looking terrific. Naw. She says, 'What's happened to you? Where have you gone? There's nothing of you left,' she says. And she looks appalled, really appalled. I feel the smile being wiped off my thin face. 'I'm jist the same auld Pat,' I say to Jenny. 'I telt ye I was going to lose it.' Jenny looks serious noo. 'Look, Pat, you've lost enough now. You look like a different person. You're losing yourself. You actually don't suit being this thin.' 'Here, you,' I says, 'this is my first night oot for ages. I don't want it starting with being told off!'

I suddenly remembered this from before. Your pals canny cope. Especially the fat ones! They feel bereft. And judged! And alone, alone in their creaking bones. 'I'm hardly a skinnymalinky longlegs,' I says to Jenny.

And I says to Jenny, 'Jist get me a sparkling water.' It feels odd being oot. I feel like I've been isolated for ages wey a long illness. Or like I've been in prison, in solitary confinement. There's quite a buzz in here. Jenny brings me a pint and a poke o' salt and vinegar. Whit can I do? Isn't it nice to have pals that know you? I mean a night out on a gless o' sparkling water is no gonna dae it fir me. I canny help but smile. 'Is Iain really gone this time?' Jenny asks. 'Aye, he's buggered off for guid this time.' 'Is that right?' Jenny says and I notices she's sort of smiling. 'Sometimes you can be lonely when you're *in* a relationship,' Jenny says. I says, 'Aye, so you can,' Jenny says, 'Pat you're a good-looking woman. Can you not just accept yourself the way you are?' I says, 'I'll accept masell when I'm down to what I want to be. This pint is a one-aff.' Jenny smiles secretively to herself, then she clinks pint glasses with me and says, 'I'll drink to you being what you want to be.' And I says, 'Cheers,' defiantly. And Jenny says, 'Cheers,' and sips the froth off her pint, studying me over her glass. She rips open the bag of crisps on the table and I feel as if a hand, not my hand, has picked up a crisp and popped it in my mouth. 'Shall I get another *poke*?' Jenny says, quite excitedly. (She puts on a Glasgow accent when she says the word poke, imitating me.) 'Naw, it's my round,' I says. 'What are you having? Same again? It's my round.' I feel like I'm on holiday. I go up to the bar and say, 'Two pints of Guinness please and two pokes of cheese and onion crisps.' It won't hurt.

Mrs Vadnie Marlene Sevlon

On the way home from a long and final day in Sunnyside Home for the Elderly, Mrs Vadnie Marlene Sevlon was relieved to notice a little breeze. Much better than yesterday when the weather was close, so close she felt the low pressure in the air. As long as there is a little breeze, a person can cope with most things – even if she is in the wrong place. It's the days when there is no breeze at all when Vadnie is convinced she made a mistake. But it wasn't like there ever seemed much choice. It wasn't like she could just take her pick. Only people with money have choice; only rich people can take their pick; everyone else must stumble from pillar to post, from hope to promise, and believe in luck and God, or maybe just God, or maybe just luck, depending on the day and the breeze. Vadnie Marlene Sevlon often said her own name, her whole name, to herself when she was alone. Perhaps because it reminded her of back home, her mother shouting *Vadnie Marlene Sevlon, come and get your dinner*, or maybe because it made her feel less lonely or maybe even just to remind herself of who she was. Time for you to get up, Vadnie Marlene Sevlon, she would say in the morning; bed for you now, Vadnie Marlene Sevlon, she would say at night. And in between the morning and the night sometimes not a single living soul said her name out loud.

Vadnie walked past the College for Boys, past the Brondesbury Park Rail Station and the Islamia Primary School, past Willesden Lane Cemetery where sometimes if she had a little time on her hands she would sit on a bench and contemplate the differences between the living and the dead. She liked to read the gravestones and imagine the lives of the fascinating names she read, and work out the ages, practising her mental arithmetic. Some people find graveyards gloomy, but not Vadnie Marlene; she felt as if she was being kept company by the peaceful dead. There was an atmosphere in Willesden Lane Cemetery that you never found in Kilburn High Street or at work or even at home. Intense contemplation! Vadnie sometimes envisaged her own headstone, though she knew nobody in her family could afford one, and anyway they wouldn't want her buried in England, and anyway she was too young to be thinking such thoughts. (She was fifty-two, hardly a spring chicken, but then not likely to be at death's door any time soon, please God. Her father was dead long time back now, but her mother was still around and living in Darling Spring, Jamaica, with three of her sisters who all wanted Vadnie to come back home. 'South of here is Grateful Hill, South West, Lucky Valley, further south then, Prospect,' her mother used

to say often, 'I'm hoping our prospects improve soon.')
But even so her mind would wander off, as it often
did, to imagining her own death, and she'd envisage
her whole name and her dates and the inscription *beloved
daughter of Gladstone and Hyacinth Sevlon, Rest in Peace,
Darling.* It wasn't perhaps what people usually did in
their lunch hours, dream up their own headstones, but
Vadnie found it quite entertaining and it passed away
the time. Should it say *passed away* or should it say *fell
asleep*, what should the exact wording be? She continued
down Salusbury Road, stopped to buy a new plug in
the DIY shop and a new packet of fuses, past the artisan
bakery, where the bread and cakes looked lovely, like
little works of art, the beauty of those breads, some so
threaded they looked like fancy hair-dos, or wiring, but
cost a small fortune, so she only ever looked in the
window; past a fancy florist where they even had birds
of paradise, which looked out of place, but cost a small
fortune so she only ever went in to the florist's to take
a deep sniff; past Queen's Park Underground Station
and right into Kilburn Lane, down Fifth Avenue, which
always made Vadnie think of New York, where she
might have gone for her contemplation, *Central Park*,
watching people skateboard, rollerblade, jog, meditate,
dance and all the things she heard say people do in
Central Park from her cousin Eldece who went over
there fifteen years ago and sometimes wrote a letter
with all her news. Eldece was maybe the lucky one. But
the strange thing about life was that you could only

live the one of them; you couldn't live the other one, the one where you went to New York instead of London, and then compare and contrast. You couldn't compare the life you had with the life you might have had though sometimes Vadnie Marlene Sevlon would have liked to be able to shout *Stop* and after the requisite minutes *Start*, and then catch the other life, live it for a bit, and if it was not as agreeable as the one in her imagination, well then she'd be able to return to the old life and appreciate it better by simply shouting *Stop* and *Start* again. As Vadnie turned into her own street, Oliphant Street, she wondered if it was luck or fate or God that made the decisions in your life. Or was it just a moment plucked from the ordinary that made you stick with mistakes already made? For instance, once, years ago, on the telephone, a man who was going to be coming to fix her electric sockets said, 'Is you Miss or Mrs?' And Vadnie answered Mrs. That was twenty years ago, when she was thirty, and was still thinking that the right man might come along. He never did but Vadnie kept the Mrs anyway. She put Mrs on her bank cards and Mrs on anything she had to sign. Mrs on her direct debits and Mrs on her television licence, Mrs on her water bill and Mrs on her gas and electric. It was Mrs Vadnie Sevlon, and she felt she got more respect that way. Strange thing was, after a number of years, she believed it herself. She was no longer surprised at the amount of post that arrived with her whole name on it. The Mrs by then didn't give her the thrill of the early days; she took it quite for granted. So might she look back on the electric man and call that fate or luck or God? Did God want her to call herself Mrs to keep herself safe from men of disrepute? When people asked her what her husband did, she would tell them he was an electrician. She would picture him vividly, combining features of the electrician with the features of a man she once sat next to on a bus to the Lake District. She made a kind of composite husband out of the two, took the hair from one and gave it to the other so he wasn't balding, just receding, took two inches of height from one and gave it to her husband, made his skin a rich dark brown. Her husband had lovely neat nails which you might not expect for an electrician. 'Oh, he works long hours; he's an electrician you see. You have to be very well qualified to be an electrician, you know. You have to know your wires, your blue and brown and black and yellow. And you need to know that blue used to be neutral, but black also used to be neutral,' Vadnie would say, whenever she got a chance, to whoever would listen, even strangers, knowledgeably quoting the most recent electrician who stood explaining his job to her for some time on the last visit to Oliphant Street. Vadnie didn't quite know what it was that made boiler men and electricity men and plumbing men always like to explain to her the exact ins and outs of what they were doing in a supremely technical way, but when an electrician came around, Vadnie listened intently. (In fact, she had found herself sometimes putting in extra plugs she didn't exactly need and could ill afford, just to be sure she was up to date.) She had to have her husband keep up with the changing times and colour codes, she couldn't have him caught short, her husband, dear Preston, Preston Sherwin Audley Sevlon; she felt such a tenderness for him. Preston: a quiet man, a man of few words, but kind deeds, whose parents were also from Jamaica but had come to England once and worked in Preston before returning to Montego Bay – well this was the story Vadnie first of all made up and later believed. When she got home from work, Preston would say, 'Put your feet up, Mrs Sevlon, and I'll make you a cup of tea.' He never raised his voice or his hand to her. He was the kind of man that is a father to daughters rather than sons, a gentle kind man, intense and protective. And of course their daughters, Ladyblossom, Marsha and Grace, were all daddy's girls. If you'd had a son, Preston would say, he would have been a mummy's boy. What would we have called a son? she heard herself asking Preston. A name after an English place, he'd say, like me, chuckling, enjoying himself, Carlisle or Kendal or Lancaster. I couldn't call a little boy Lancaster, she'd find herself saying out loud in the kitchen – then startle herself with his absence. Was it luck that got her the job as a care home orderly at Sunnyside Home for the Elderly? Or was she being deliberately led down the wrong path? It was only two days a week but it seemed like a beginning in the beginning. And she well remembered the first day all that time ago, why, it must be fifteen years at least, walking down the driveway and glimpsing the garden with the bench, the table with the green umbrella, thinking the place was really something quite, quite special. The grounds were grand and made her feel she was definitely in England. They were a people that knew how to make a garden, the English! And during the first few weeks Vadnie would eat her Coronation chicken sandwich in the palatial garden with the blossom on the trees and the green grass under her feet and feel almost content; at least, the worry about money and the future would lift and she would be in the unusual position of just being able to sit and eat her sandwich and watch the birds flit about in the trees. She always kept her eye out for a Barbuda warbler even though she didn't think they ever came to this country. But if birds of paradise could be in the florist then Barbuda warblers could be in the garden. It would have lifted her heart to see a bird from back home in the garden of Sunnyside Home for the Elderly. She didn't much like the two women who ran Sunnyside, and they didn't get any better over time. For a start they had no sense of humour, which was quite a problem. Vadnie had never realized how big a problem this could be until she first ran into the two sad Sunnyside women. All the good conversation has to have a little light-ness! Well, the first thing Vadnie said to the matron was, 'The garden is quite something. What lovely borders!

You do all the weeding yourself?' (Of course she was joking, and was going to go on to mention the beautiful garden design, but the matron – she didn't get it.) She replied seriously, snooty-like, 'No, no. We have a gardener.' Just like that. And Vadnie nodded, undaunted, and said, 'Handsome man is he, this gardener? About my age do you think?' Matron stared and said, 'He's Irish,' as if that might be something that would put Vadnie off. 'And he's in his seventies.' That would be the clincher, then. So after that Vadnie never joked with Matron, which meant there was no basis for conversation; there was only a way of receiving instructions. And the head nurse was even worse. She had something nasty about her, that woman, and no mistake. She was always picking fault. She'd say to Vadnie, 'Did you *say* you had washed the kitchen floor?' when the floor was gleaming, gleaming, so shiny Vadnie could see her face in it, which was the test her mother had given her when she was a little girl. She would say, *Have you polished so bright you can see your reflection?* Whenever Vadnie did see her reflection in some domestic surface, it never looked like her, and she'd have to pause for a minute and say, *Is that me, is that really me?* Sometimes she loomed in things. She appeared all out of proportion.

Still it is not an absolute necessity to get on with the people you work for, especially not when they are your boss. When you do get on with them, they can let you down even more. Vadnie remembered the woman she cleaned for in St Elizabeth in Jamaica saying, 'Very sorry, Vads, but you're no longer needed. You did such an excellent job and have been like family to us, but . . .' And what was the real reason? The details of the thing had gone, but the hurt was still there. That was the interesting thing about hurt. All the vocabulary can go, all the words said and heard, and yet the pain persists in your heart, slow and heavy. The worst hurts were wordless, or at least they became wordless. A lot of the old people in Sunnyside Home for the Elderly didn't speak, or if they did speak they didn't make that much sense. They seemed in their own world, a lost world, a vanquished world. They didn't have many places like this back home. The family took the elderly in and that was that. Imagine the planning: building these big houses to incarcerate all the old mummies and daddies, imagine the spreadsheets and architectural blueprints, to hide away all the old grandparents. Imagine inventing these places for them. Even if Sunnyside did have a nice garden, it was still a kind of hell. All of the grandmas and grandpas lined up to look out of the window! They were never allowed out to take a little stroll. Once Vadnie asked Matron if she could take a stroll with one of the women, Margaret, and Matron said, We are not insured to allow them to walk about in the garden. Would you pay if she fell over? Would you pay all the damages? Something like that. Vadnie said, Yes, it'll be fine, she won't fall over, she is quite steady on her feet. But Matron shook her head and said, So you think I'm paying you to go strolling around the garden? You must think I was born yesterday. Vadnie stopped to consider this seriously for a moment, the idea that the matron could be born yesterday and then grow in such a short space of time into such a nasty old woman. Not possible! Nastiness needs time to build up.

Today the morning had started with Vadnie saying to herself, Time to get up, Vadnie Marlene Sevlon. Preston was up and out and had not brought her the usual cup of hot tea. The girls had already grown up and left home. Grace was the first in the family at university. Sometimes, she'd find herself doing a big shop and telling people the family was coming home, that's why her trolley was suddenly loaded. Today nobody was there and nobody was coming home and she felt suddenly tired. Odd times at the Sunnyside Home for the Elderly, she'd found herself having to take a ten-pound note or two to help her get by because they didn't pay her enough and because the old people were not going anywhere anyway and none of them would miss it and because she was the only one in the place who was kind so deserved it and because she tried to do good things with it, often buying them little treats, and sometimes even buying them clothes. But today the day didn't feel right from the word go. When she arrived in Sunnyside, Margaret, her favourite of the old people and the most with-it and the one who took the most interest in Preston and the girls, implored her to buy her a cherry red cardigan. She was in some distress. 'Would you manage to buy me a red cardigan,' she asked, her voice shrill, anxious. 'I'll try my best,' Vadnie found herself saying. 'Tell me your size.' And Margaret looked happy, happy as she'd ever seen her. She was sure that the matron and the other one didn't treat them well; Vadnie thought they might even be abusive but she never saw anything with her own eyes. Recently, though, she had made heavy hints about the authorities, and she had sat at home glued to a documentary about a whistleblower. (She had never heard the term before.) 'I might blow the whistle,' Vadnie had thought to herself. 'Tell me,' Vadnie said to Margaret quietly, 'won't you tell me if they ever lay a finger on you?' Maybe one of them overheard; Vadnie didn't know how it had all started. But at the end of the day that had started strangely, Vadnie found herself dismissed. After twenty years: dismissed. And the thing that distressed her most was that she wouldn't be able to return with Margaret's cherry red cardigan. She wouldn't be able to tell Margaret how Preston was, how Ladyblossom, Grace and Marsha were doing. They might as well all be dead.

On the way home Vadnie felt the breeze on her face and the strange feeling turning into Oliphant Street that violence was in the air. She walked slowly, heavily. She had a tight feeling across her chest. She was sweating. She stopped in the DIY shop and bought a new plug and a new packet of fuses. 'My husband used to be an electrician,' she told the woman, 'yet could I get him to fix a plug?' The woman in the shop laughed. 'Mine is a carpenter – ditto!' She paused. 'You said "used to",' the woman said. Vadnie nodded slowly, 'Yes, he passed away a few weeks ago. He's buried up the road there in Willesden Cemetery.' 'Oh, I'm sorry,' the woman said. Mrs Vadnie Marlene Sevlon dabbed at the sudden tears falling down her face. 'He was a good man, a terribly good man,' she said.

The Winter Visitor

I can almost see her: she is standing by the window looking out at the snow falling. She looks at her watch. It is January. She puts some lip gloss on her lips so that they don't crack in the eight below freezing temperature outside. Though it is night time now, and the moon is blurred behind the snow fog, she puts on her thick, grim coat, long gloves, hat and boots. There is nothing I can do or say that will stop her coming. She wants to be here by morning, before I'm even awake. Her suitcase is already packed, a small hard suitcase with a few clothes for her stay. Though she plans to stay for months, she has packed very little: very few toiletries, just a toothbrush and a comb, a few pairs of knickers, tights and a couple of long thick skirts. She smiles a tight dry smile. She is coming for me and there is nothing I can do.

She walks through the night, carrying her suitcase. She has an almost uncanny sense of balance, and so the slipperiness of the snow does not faze her as it would me. She walks with the determination of someone on a mission, up through Rushholme, turns right into Pratt Lane, turns left into the Princess Parkway, turns right into Mauldeth Road, turns right again into Barlow Moor Road. Her long boots have good grips. She knows she is close. She can see her own breath flare out of her mouth. She's come to me before, so the streets, even in the snow and the snow-lit dark are not new to her. Over the years, she's come like this, no planning, no date in the diary. She just turns up – first thing in the morning – punctual and precise. The last time was three years ago, and I was certain then, when she left, that I'd never see her again. Perhaps she enjoys the fact that she comes unannounced; she's terribly arrogant. It's difficult to tell because she says very little. Maybe the interesting question is why I have her, why I let it happen, time and time again. I genuinely don't know the answer.

I wake. That's something I suppose, I wake. I wake though I'm not sure if I've slept. I've been in and out of the ether all night, and quite a few times I got up and looked out into my street. One time I saw a black cat walk across the street. It looked so black in the white snow. It looked like it owned the place. Another time I got up for a glass of water. I'd clearly drunk a whole glass already but had no memory of doing so. Another time I stared at a pile of books and tried to read their titles. I've not eaten anything since I've woken. I know I should get up. But my body feels heavy, leaden, and I can't manage it. I try and sit up, and pull a book from the bedside table, but the words swim in front of my eyes and I can't read. None of it makes any sense. I'm starting to feel frightened. I daren't call my mother because she will recognize the thick sound in my voice, the sound of my own fear. I don't want to talk to anybody. I'd like them all to leave me alone.

When I wake again, I know she is in the house. I sit up in my bed and listen. There are noises down stairs, a battering of saucepans and a clattering of cutlery. She knows this sort of noise sets my teeth on edge. I fold my pillow over the top of my head so that it covers both ears. I can scarcely breathe. The truth is I'm terrified of her. I know that with her arrival, nothing will be possible. She won't let me out to see friends; she won't let me use the telephone; she won't let me read, or let me sleep. She seems to already have me doing her work just before she gets here, because yesterday I found reading difficult, I think. It's all a sort of jumble. She is fanatical about sorting out cupboards, but we both know it is not to do with order. There are other motives, stranger and more difficult to pinpoint.

I take the pillow off my head and listen carefully. I can hear nothing. The house is as silent as snow. It's cold,

very cold, even underneath the duvet, and it is early.
I look at the face of the clock on my bedside table. It
says it is seven in the morning. Why does she insist on
coming so early when she knows I'm a late riser? The
whole day is stretched out ahead like a field of frozen
snow. The banging starts up again. I ought to get up
and go down the stairs and confront her, but I can't. I
try lifting a leg and pulling myself around, but I can't
make it. I lift my leg back under the covers. The only
place is the bed, and the wall facing the bed. The only
thing when she comes is to lie still, and quiet with my
face to the wall. I can keep it up for the longest time,
while she is downstairs, pulling things out of the cellar,
yanking cupboards and cabinets open and chucking
things away. Last time she came, she found a box of
my old love letters and shredded them. I don't think
she even wants me to have a past. A time ago, I found
out my lover was unfaithful. It only takes one infidelity
to alter the landscape of love beyond all recognition.
Frankly, it was a relief she shredded the lying *love you,
love you, love you*, but she wasn't to know that.

I don't really care what she does when she comes.
Perhaps she is trying to get me interested. I've noticed
that the wallpaper in this bedroom is thick and that
when she comes I'm prone to peeling little bits back.
The other thing I do is picking at my lips. In this
weather my lips chap easily and so the constant peeling

them does not help, but I can't stop. I find my hand there and I try and take it away. I wonder how long it will be before she comes up here and says something. She's got a nerve, coming in and going straight for the utensils. I hear the kettle whistle. I'm not hungry which is just as well. The sight of her takes away my appetite. There's something so appalling about her features. It is not too much to say they revolt me. I despise her. There. I've said it. I despise her; her long skirts, her long back, her grim smile. She is an abomination.

I hear her feet on the stairs. There's nowhere for me to go and I can't get up. I hide under the covers listening to her footsteps getting closer and closer. She is coming for me. If I could shout Help I would. If I knew shouting Help might help I would. I hear my bedroom door open. It needs oil, the door. I live in a house that frightens me and I have not even done the simplest of things to stop myself being frightened. I have not bought oil for the door. I know I should struggle up so that at least I am in a sitting position, but I can't. 'Get up,' she says. 'Sit up.' I lie cowering under the sheets. Three years. I feel so disappointed. She pulls my duvet back. 'Sit up. You must eat. I've brought you some porridge.' She helps pull me up and I stare at her blankly. 'You must eat.' She puts the tray down beside me. She knows I don't like her porridge, cooked with salt and not with sugar. 'I will feed you if you won't feed yourself,' she says.

And she is not joking. The last time, she sat across

my chest and force-fed me. She sits at the edge of the bed, waiting. Slowly, I pick up a spoon and try and shovel some of the sludge into my mouth. Some people have no food, she says. Some old people are snowed in and have no food at all. Get that down you. She looks at me with total contempt. It is hard to swallow. It is the most terrible thing. 'How long have you come for?' I ask her. I can't stop my voice trembling. 'I've come for as long as it takes,' she says. 'I never come for any less than it takes,' she says enunciating each word as if English was a foreign language to her. 'For what?' 'I'm here now. It's a little late for that.' She walks to my bedroom windows and yanks open the curtains. The daylight advances without mercy. Soon she will tell me I'm lucky to have a roof over my head. The snow is bright on the ground, thick. There's a pinkish light where the sun hits the snow. 'Later, we must walk out in the snow. You have boots?' 'I can't go out,' I say. 'I can't go out.' 'Drink your tea,' she says. 'I have let you have a sugar. We will see later about going out on a walk. You will see the snow on the trees and the frozen lake. Down the hill, there are people sledging on FOR SALE signs. There's the recession for you. You are lucky to have a roof over your head.' She hasn't changed in three years. Her hair has some grey in it, but so does mine. We are both middle-aged now. Her face is perhaps a little more lined. There's a tightness around her lips and eyes. Just looking at her makes my skin tingle, my chest heave, my heart heavy. Behind the sockets of my eyes are small barrels full of salt water. My eyes are stinging. I feel so full of regret. What is wrong with me that I cannot assert myself.

When I've eaten as much of her porridge as I can, she picks up the tray and says, 'You should wash now.' I find myself in the bathroom with a cloth; I find my hand taking the cloth over my face. She's standing behind me and I can see her reflection in the mirror. 'Good,' she says. 'The cold water is best. Don't forget teeth!' I look at my toothbrush holder with some horror. Her toothbrush is already in there along with the paste she likes, the fennel toothpaste. Her small black toilet bag is on the floor next to the sink. It contains a razor, and an Elastoplast. I know that she regularly shaves her moustache, from the marks left around her top lip.

She had planned to make me take a walk today, but she underestimated how heavy my limbs are. I managed down the stairs and I waded into the kitchen. I opened my cupboards and saw that she had rearranged my jars of treacle and honey, and ordered my spices. I looked inside my bread bin and saw that she had tidied it up. 'Your kitchen is a mess,' she said, matter-of-factly. 'You have all these spices – cardamom, cumin, coriander, chilli, paprika . . . Yet I don't ever see you cook.' 'I don't cook when you are here,' I say to her, right to her tight, dour face. I don't need to speak behind her long back. 'I wouldn't cook for you if my life depended on it.' I would rather be dead than have her descend on me. 'Who do you think you are to turn up here and sort out my cupboards?' She shrugs and smiles her fixed smile, pleased to have got a reaction from me. 'It's hardly a crime, cleaning your cupboards,' she says. 'Besides you deserved it.'

It is a long time I think since she first arrived, though I can't be sure. One day has slid into the next, and the snow is still here, covering everything. There have been extra inches of it fluttering and floating to the ground, every day she has made me eat her porridge, her soup and her stew. She is not a good cook; she seems to take pleasure in serving up gruel. Every day she has dressed in more or less the same clothes, heavy long tweed skirts, wool tights, polo neck jumpers and cardigans. I can see she has grown to depend on looking after me. I'm going to have some trouble kicking her out. I wonder who I could ring to get rid of her. It occurs to me that you can ring all sorts of people to get rid of all sorts of things from your house: cockroaches, wasps, bluebottles, wood lice, mice, rats, burglars, fire. But I have no one to ring to get rid of her. What would I say if I called the police exactly? There is a woman claiming to know me who has moved into my house and is making me eat porridge every day? I would sound ridiculous. Even I know that. There's nothing I can do except wait for her to shift of her own accord.

At least now that she has unpacked and settled in

and been here for two weeks or is it three, maybe even four, I'm not so scared of her. She makes me come down to the table to eat the meals, and when I come into the kitchen she stands up, and rubs her hands together. 'Good. Now we will eat,' she says. And we eat in silence. We don't do anything else. Sometimes I go through to the living room and we sit on the sofa and stare at the wall together in a most companionable fashion. 'There is absolutely nothing on television,' she says every day. 'And anyway you don't want to become a couch potato.'

One day I ask her where she comes from. Where does she live when she is not living with me? But she refuses to answer personal questions, though I imagine she is from a cold place, a very cold place, since these extremes don't bother her at all. Today, she says, I insist that we go for a walk. She ties a scarf around my neck and buttons my coat, as if I were incapable of doing these things for myself. 'I am not a child,' I say. 'I am a middle-aged woman.' 'You certainly could have fooled me,' she says, and for the first time I see a real smile on her face, and catch a glimpse of her teeth.

'If you don't walk, I will carry you on my back like a sack of potatoes,' she says. This amuses me because although she is taller than me, she is much slimmer, and I weigh thirteen stone and four pounds. Her arms are strong looking and full of muscle. I picture me being carried across her back through the snow like a bag of coal or a sack of potatoes or a dead body heading

for a mortuary. I choose to walk. She opens the front
door and there it is: the freezing cold air. 'Minus nine
today,' she says, almost cheerfully. We brace the bitter
wind together. She even loops her arm through mine.
We go as far as Chorlton Park. The school is closed.
In the park are huge snow penises and massive snow
men, but the penises are the surprise, I've never seen
one before, a snow penis, complete with balls and
everything. She stares at me staring at it. 'You've never
seen one before?' she asks me. 'No,' I say. 'Never.' She
laughs, and her laugh has a trill to it, like a little frill
on the end of a serious skirt. 'You haven't lived,' she
says. I realize she has quite a sense of humour; when
I'm with her I can see the absurd things in life. There
are lots of birds on the trees in the park, robin red-
breasts and other birds whose names I forget. 'So many
birds will die,' she says sadly. 'Can we feed them?' I
say. 'Can we go and get some bird feed?' She looks at
me astonished, as if I'd asked her if we could fly to the
moon. 'Can we go and get some bird feed?' she echoes.
I nod. 'It is early for you to be asking such a question,'
she says, sounding a little sad. 'What do you mean?' I
say. But she doesn't reply. She trudges with me through
the thick snow. I hate the thought of the birds dying
because of the snow. The snow lies on the fields in the
park and it looks blameless, implacable, like it would
never admit to anything, to tripping anyone up or
trapping an old person in a house.

We walk along Barlow Moor Road till we come to

the shop opposite the post office. 'We can get bird feed here,' she says, softly. 'You go.' 'On my own?' I ask her. 'Yes, of course. You can do it.' Her eyes are welling up. When I come out with a bag of seed for wild birds in my hands, she is gone. I can't see her anywhere. I stand waiting for a while, thinking she might have gone to post a letter. Then I cross the road and look in the post office, but she isn't there. The last time she came, I remember she disappeared just as suddenly. Odd behaviour, really. I make it home, alone. I listen in the hall just in case she's come home early to test me. I look for her in the kitchen; she might be putting the kettle on for our tea. I go upstairs to check she hasn't started on the bathroom cupboards. The last time she came she did them. But no, she is nowhere, nowhere to be seen. I don't know what to feel. I don't feel relief. I feel something more complicated than that. I look out my bedroom window to see if I might see her in the street. Something puzzles me. There is no snow on the ground at all.

Acknowledgements

Some of these stories have been published in *Granta*, the *Sunday Herald*, and the *Independent on Sunday*. Others have been broadcast on BBC Radio 4. 'Mind Away' was commissioned by Sky Arts and shown in a dramatized version as part of the *Theatre Live* Series. 'The First Lady of Song' was commissioned by Glyndebourne and was first published in *Midsummer Nights* (ed. Jeanette Winterson). 'Hadassah' was formed as part of the 66 writers retelling the Bible and was performed at the Bush Theatre. 'Reality, Reality' came from a joint commission by Aye Write and the Scots Malt Whisky Society. 'The White Cot' was partly inspired by Charlotte Perkins Gillman's *The Yellow Wallpaper*.

A very big thank you to Kate Harvey, Camilla Elworthy, Sarah Chalfant, Catherine Marcangeli, Nick Drake and Ali Smith.